Eileen
59

*The teachers of
the law and the
Pharisees brought in a
woman caught in adultery.
They made her stand before the
group and said to Jesus, "Teacher,
this woman was caught in the
act of adultery."*

—JOHN 8:3–4 (NIV)

*"The LORD your God is with you, the
Mighty Warrior who saves. He will take
great delight in you; in his love he will
no longer rebuke you, but will rejoice
over you with singing."*

—ZEPHANIAH 3:17 (NIV)

Ordinary Women of the BIBLE

✦

Ordinary Women of the BIBLE

NO STONE CAST

ELIYANAH'S STORY

Carole Towriss

Guideposts

Danbury, Connecticut

Ordinary Women of the BIBLE

❖

NO STONE CAST
CAST
ELIYANAH'S STORY

Dedication

To every woman who longs to hear
the voice of God singing over her

Cast of
CHARACTERS

Eleazar (Ezi) • brother of Miriam and Marta. Better known by the Greek version of his name, Lazarus. (fictional: son of Simeon)

Eliyanah (Yana) • woman accused of adultery

Marta • sister of Miriam and Eleazar. Better known by the Greek version of her name: Martha. (fictional: daughter of Simeon)

Miriam • sister of Marta and Eleazar. Better known by the Greek version of her name, Mary. (fictional: daughter of Simeon)

Simeon • a man of Bethany who contracted tsara'at and was healed. Better known by the Greek version of his name, Simon. (Fictional: father of Miriam, Marta, and Eleazar)

Fictional

Abihu, Amariah • young sons of Elon and Basya

Adira • daughter of Ketziah

Alexander (Xander) • servant of Oded, brother of Diana

Basya • wife of Elon

Benaiah • father of Naomi and one of the priests of the Sanhedrin

Dalya • wet nurse of Sarai

Deborah • mother of Eliyanah

Diana • servant of Oded, sister of Xander

Elisheba, Elizabeth, Rachel, Susannah • residents of Bethany

Elon • younger brother of Oded

Gavriel • young son of Adira

Hannah, Rada • residents of the bet in Bethany

Ketziah • yarn merchant, mother of Adira

Kronos • husband of Sopha

Lemuel • stepfather of Yana

Naomi • mother of Oded and Elon

Oded • husband of Eliyanah

Sarai • daughter of Oded and Yana

Sopha • servant of Oded

Glossary of
TERMS

Ancient Hebrew

abba • father

ba'al, *m.* (**ba'alah, ba'ali** *f., poss.*) • master (mistress, my master)

bet • house

Hallel • a portion of the service for certain Jewish festivals, consisting of Psalms 113–118.

imma • mother

mohar • money given by the groom to the family of the bride, originally intended to be used in purchasing goods for the newlyweds and in securing the future financial independence of the bride. This money was often given to the bride as a dowry.

motek • sweetheart

Pesach • Passover

sabba • grandfather

shalom • peace, a greeting or parting phrase

Sukkot • Festival of Tabernacles

tsara'at • an unknown disfiguring skin disease; also mold in clothing or houses (mistranslated as leprosy). It is not the same as what we call leprosy or Hansen's disease.

INTRODUCTION

The story of the woman caught in adultery is one of the most controversial in all of scripture. I didn't know that when I decided to write about her.

Most scholars believe the incident actually happened, but most also believe the passage doesn't belong in this section of John's Gospel. They think it was removed by earlier church leaders who feared it might give the impression Christ condoned adultery when He told the woman, "Go, and sin no more."

In antiquity, "adultery" referred to a married or betrothed woman having sexual relations with someone other than her husband. A husband could be unfaithful, and as long as the woman was not someone else's wife, it was not considered adultery.

Jewish law and customs decreed that at least two witnesses—not including the husband—had to see the woman actually engaging in sexual relations. It seems clear that this woman was indeed guilty.

However, if a husband suspected his wife of infidelity, he was not to set her up to be caught but instead take her to the priests to undergo the ordeal of bitter waters, which could take several months (Numbers 5). He could also take the much faster route of simply divorcing her.

God's law was meant to make marriage sacred and permanent. When Moses said a man could divorce his wife by writing a certificate of divorce, this was actually meant to make divorce more difficult. Because the husband had to have a good reason, he had to take the time to go to a legal authority and have a document drawn up, and unless he could prove she'd been unfaithful, he had to allow her to keep her dowry so she had money to live on.

By the time of Jesus, the Law delivered by Moses had been interpreted, expanded upon, debated, and often twisted beyond recognition. The Pharisees said it was legal for a husband to divorce his wife for burning his dinner, growing older, or even being too noisy. Women addressed their husbands as "lord" or "master."

A woman's place was literally in the home, bearing and raising children. Many leaders taught that a woman should never leave the home except to go to the synagogue. Others permitted her to go to the market. She was also allowed to visit her family, especially for weddings and funerals.

A devout man would not speak to or even greet a woman in public. Men were "sons of Abraham," but women were not referred to as his daughters. Women were forbidden to study the Torah. Any money a woman earned belonged to her husband.

From birth to death, a woman was always under the authority of a man: her father, her husband, or a male relative of her husband if she was a widow.

In contrast, Jesus called women "Daughter." He listened to them, spoke to them in public, healed them. He treated them with respect and compassion. He accepted women as His disciples and taught them the scriptures. Women were the first witnesses to the resurrection.

Jesus refused to see women as "less than" but made it clear He valued them, cherished them, loved them.

He was nothing less than radical.

CHAPTER ONE

I will get up now and go about the city,
through its streets and squares;
I will search for the one my heart loves.

~ Song of Songs 3:2 ~

Month of Tammuz
Early Summer, AD 30
Bethany, Judea

*B*et-ani. *House of Afflictions.* That's what people called her village.

For Eliyanah, it was a place of joy. Of family. Of love.

The place she would marry her best friend and spend her life with him.

From the rooftop of her small stone and mud-brick house, she looked out over the tiny village of Bethany, still shrouded in dusky, gray light. She sucked in a lungful of fresh morning air. The Mount of Olives lay to the northwest, the desert valley to the east. Birdsong filled the air. The fragrance of ripening apple and grape blossoms rode a gentle breeze. Towering date palms hovered over the nearly dry river beyond the village's walls.

Life in Bethany was perfect.

Thank Adonai no one else was awake this early, because Yana could not hide the smile that threatened to burst from deep within and erupt in laughter. Her heart pounded and her breathing quickened.

Her beloved would return to Bethany today.

She silently rolled up her mat and laid it against the ledge of the packed-dirt roof. Careful not to awaken her *imma*—or Imma's husband—she climbed down the ladder that led to a large square room below, the center section open to the brilliant blue sky. One third housed their sheep in the rainy season, not only to protect the animal but to add its warmth to cold nights when the family slept inside.

The other two thirds contained a cistern filled with water from the river, sleeping benches built into the wall, and pegs to hold extra tunics. A small beehive-shaped bread oven, unused in summer, sat next to a cold firepit.

She retrieved the jar of barley she'd ground yesterday and stepped outside into the courtyard they shared with her *abba's* cousin Simeon and his children. Kneeling by the large common oven, she poked at the embers, stirring them to life. She placed dried grass on top to encourage a flame and then added dung. When a bright orange fire flared, she poured crushed grain into a bowl and added water and salt, forming circular, flat loaves.

As she absently slapped the rounds of dough to the side of the oven, one after another, she tried to keep her mind from focusing on her beloved's soft brown eyes. The feel of his hand in hers. The low voice that sent a chill down her spine when he whispered in her ear.

After removing each loaf when it had cooked to a deep golden brown, she replaced it with another round of uncooked dough and soon had a stack of hot bread.

She grabbed four of the flatbreads and hurried to the broadroom that ran along the back of the house, where she searched the pottery jars that lined the shelves. She poured out a handful of last year's dates then placed them in a sack along with a chunk of sheep's milk cheese, a bunch of fresh grapes, and the bread, and tied a string around it.

The sun now hovered fully above the horizon. It wouldn't be long now. She slipped out the door, hurried through the courtyard, and headed for the gate.

"Yana!"

Just outside the gate she froze and suppressed a sigh. She'd hoped to avoid her cousin Miriam. Yana didn't want to explain why she was rushing to meet Miriam's younger brother.

"Going somewhere?" She smiled. Miriam was only a year or two older than Yana, but Yana always felt like a child in her presence.

"I was hoping to catch you. Can you take this to Eleazar as well?" She handed Yana a small package.

"Well, um..." How did she explain this?

Miriam pulled back one corner of the cloth to reveal two handfuls of pistachios, already shelled. "He loves them, but he can't sit still long enough to eat them." She laughed.

Yana frowned. "That's all?" Not a big meal for someone who had spent the last two weeks with the village's sheep and goats, leading them to fresh grass and water.

Miriam smiled. "I thought you'd be bringing him the rest." She glanced down at the bag at Yana's side.

She knew? How did she find out? They'd been so careful.

"You may have kept it a secret, but he couldn't. Sisters notice when their baby brother wanders around the house smiling for no reason whatsoever."

Oh no. Her ears began to burn.

"Everyone knows, though no one has said anything. Even Abba knows. I'm thrilled. I can't think of anyone better for him than you."

Warmth spread from her chest all over her body. "Truly?"

"Truly. I'd be delighted to have you as a sister." She leaned in and kissed Yana's cheek, then spun around and returned to her house.

Yana placed the pistachios in the bag and hurried along the village's only road toward the northern edge of the village.

She reached the common sheepfold that lay just beyond the last house in the shadow of the tree-covered mountain. In the dry season, all the animals remained together outside the village, and younger girls and boys took turns leading them to the green pastures and cool water in the hills. Eleazar could have given up his turn years ago, but he loved the time alone, wandering in the hills.

She waited, pacing, moving the bag from one fist to the other while keeping an eye on the dirt path that led to Jerusalem.

She heard the sheep before she saw him. She adjusted her head cloth, tucked a stray strand of hair behind her ear, and smoothed her tunic.

And waited.

Finally, his lanky form sauntered down the path, crook in one hand, the sheep following behind him.

Her heartbeat doubled, and she started down the road toward him.

Eleazar's face lit up as she approached. He paused, the flock parting and swooshing past on either side of the couple toward the fold.

She halted before him. "Good morning, Ezi."

He smiled softly. "I love it when you call me that."

When she'd first moved here with Imma, he was eight or nine years old. But she'd only begun to talk, and she couldn't get her tongue to pronounce his name. To her he became Ezi, and even now she rarely called him by his proper name. "Did you sleep well last night?"

A sly grin crossed his face. "Of course. I dreamed of you."

Her cheeks heated. "You can't say things like that."

"Why not? We're going to be married, aren't we?"

"Not unless you speak to Lemuel." She grinned.

"I should probably bathe first, don't you think? I just returned from two weeks with the sheep and goats." He laughed. "I'll do it tonight, I promise."

He glanced quickly at the empty landscape surrounding them, then leaned nearer, his warm breath caressing her cheek. "I missed you."

"I missed you too. I'm glad you're home."

He took her hand and they strolled back toward the village. Just as they reached the last house along the road, Simeon stopped them, his face twisted.

Ezi halted. "Abba, what's wrong?"

Simeon fixed his eyes on her. "Yana, I'm sorry to tell you. Your abba—"

"He is *not* my father." She tried to keep her voice respectful, difficult as it was.

"I know, but he is your imma's husband, and according to the law, he has an abba's authority over you."

"And?" Ezi's voice was sharp.

"He has betrothed you to a man in Jerusalem."

The words ripped through her soul. *No!*

She tried to understand. The message was simple—only a handful of words. But no matter how hard she tried, no matter how many times she turned the sentence over in her mind, it didn't make sense.

Lemuel knew she loved Eleazar. He knew Simeon approved of the match.

"But why?" She searched Simeon's eyes, seeking an answer. An explanation. A reason.

"I'm so sorry, Yana. Your ab—Lemuel has decided. There is nothing I, or anyone, can do."

Ezi turned to her, agony written on his face. "What about your imma?"

"You know exactly what she will say. She would never contradict him."

Life as she knew it, as she had hoped and dreamed it would be, was over.

Yana let the courtyard gate slam behind her and marched toward her house on the left side of the courtyard.

"Yana! Back so soon?" Imma stepped out from the broad-room, a jar in hand.

"You *knew*! You knew and you let me go to him. How... Why? Why didn't you tell me?"

Imma blanched. "Who told you?"

"Simeon."

Her face clouded. "He should have waited. It was not his place to share our news."

"He did it because he cares about me! And Ezi." She stomped around the lower floor.

"I care about you too. More than you realize." She reached for Yana's shoulder, but Yana recoiled.

"Then why make me marry someone I've never met? Never heard of? When you know Ezi and I've been talking about it."

Imma's brows furrowed. "You know I had no say."

"I know you could have a say if you wanted. But you're so afraid he'll leave us. Like my abba did."

"That's enough. Lemuel will leave for his vineyards any mo—" Imma shot a glance toward the ladder.

Lemuel already stood at the bottom, arms crossed. He was an imposing man, taller than most, with broad

7

shoulders, thinning hair, and dark eyes that never seemed to smile.

He glanced from Imma to Yana then back to Imma. "Deborah. You told her."

Imma took a step back, her hands up. "No. I wouldn't. You kno—"

"But she somehow found out." He glared at Yana.

"You know there is no such thing as a secret in this village." She held his gaze. No use trying to be nice to him anymore, trying to be polite and respectful so he'd allow her to marry Ezi.

He shrugged. "So you know. Saves me telling you."

"But—"

"No!"

Yana cringed at his shout.

He shook a long, thick finger at her. "There will be no discussion. He is my kinsman, and I've already begun the negotiations. Besides, he is better than you deserve."

The words hit her like a slap in the face. Better than she deserved?

"I've taken care of you for the last six years. Longer than your own abba stuck around." He snorted. "What do you think would have happened to you and your imma had I not married her? Do you think anyone else would have done what I did, marrying a divorced woman with another man's child to raise?" He sneered. "Of course not. One man had already left her. There must have been a reason. No one else would take that chance."

Yana watched Imma's face as he ranted. Imma hung her head. She believed every word this man said. She always had.

"So you will do as you're told. It's your duty to do what is best for the family. This match will help us all."

"How? How does this help us *all*?"

"He is a powerful, respected merchant, a dealer in spices. He has ties with the priests, with other merchants. He has a spacious house with many servants. He is quite wealthy, and he will see that you are well provided for."

"And how does this help *you*?"

"That is not your concern."

"Enormous bridewealth? Is that how it benefits you?"

He stepped nearer, stopping an arm's length away. His dark eyes glared down at her.

Perhaps she had gone too far.

"Yes, he is gifting us with a *mohar* beyond what someone like you could ever expect." His voice was low, controlled. "But even I, as any good abba would, will give most of it to you for your dowry." He turned and left, heading to check on his vineyards.

Imma sat on the sleeping bench built into the wall and patted the space beside her. "Eliyanah, sit down. I need to explain something to you."

Imma's face was calm, but her words frightened Yana. "Imma?"

"Please, just sit."

Yana did as she was told.

"When your father left us, when he *abandoned* us after moving us here from Galilee, my dowry should have remained with me. Although a dowry is meant to be kept by the woman, the husband is allowed to use it as he sees fit, as long as it can be returned to her should he die or divorce her without cause." Imma took her hand. "But your abba had lost ours. We had nothing. You know what could have happened to us. To me. We only survived because his cousin helped us."

She knew. Widows and divorced women led precarious lives in Israel. Those with no family support could easily end up in prostitution. Had it not been for Simeon...

Imma cupped Yana's cheeks with wrinkled palms. "If Lemuel had not married me—" She smiled weakly. "He does care for you, in his own way."

Perhaps. As long as it didn't hurt *him*.

"I want you protected. I don't want to be worrying about you when—" She clamped her mouth shut. "When I'm old and unable to do anything about it."

"But Ezi—"

"My precious daughter, it's rare when a woman can marry for love. Those of little means marry for survival, of themselves and of the family. Even daughters of kings and priests marry to form alliances, to enhance the status of their family." She shrugged. "This man is one of the most successful merchants in all Jerusalem. He could be very useful to Lemuel, and it's important to him to make these connections. What's important to *me* is that you are protected. This man can do both."

Any hope she had of changing Imma's mind flickered and went out. "Yes, Imma."

Imma rose and began to pace. "This man—his name is Oded—is willing to gift us with bridewealth far more than anyone else could and more than we have a right to expect. Otherwise I would have nothing to give you."

Yana shook her head. "I don't care about that. I am very happy as we are."

"But I care. I don't want you to struggle as I have, ever."

Imma had made up her mind. She saw this marriage as a means to a good and secure life for Yana. She firmly believed she was doing what was best for Yana.

Perhaps she was right.

CHAPTER TWO

There will always be poor people in the land.
Therefore I command you to be openhanded
toward your fellow Israelites who are
poor and needy in your land.

~ Deuteronomy 15:11 ~

Those who passed through Bethany on their way from Jerusalem to Jericho noticed only the almshouse the Essenes had set up generations ago.

And of course, the notorious caves.

At least most of them left behind a gift to help the village continue caring for the poor and ill. Spending time at the large house near the center of the village was the best part of Yana's day, but first she had to help her cousins Miriam and Marta prepare the day's bread.

A week had passed since Simeon had delivered the message that would change her life. She'd shoved the thought deep in the back of her mind, refusing to give it life. Betrothals usually lasted a year. That provided plenty of time for the bride and groom to prepare.

Yana munched on a piece of leftover bread. The sun already poured its heat over the land though it had risen but little. The air was stagnant and dry, and the colorful wildflowers that had dotted the landscape in spring had all withered.

Imma stepped outside to join her.

"Good morning, Imma. Did you sleep well?"

"Well enough. I don't sleep much at my age."

Yana eyed her. There were dark circles under her eyes. She walked as if she carried the weight of the world on her slender shoulders and as if she was ready to give up.

"Do you need anything before I go?"

Imma smiled. "No, go. They need you."

Yana leaned near to place a quick kiss on Imma's cheek. "I'll be back to eat the midday meal with you and get the stew started," she called over her shoulder as she rushed across the courtyard toward Simeon's house.

The sound of stone scraping against stone mixed with plodding donkey steps was always calming to Yana. Miriam walked beside the lumbering animal as it circled the mill. Without it, it would take all day to produce enough flour to feed everyone at the house.

"*Shalom.*" Without looking up, Miriam poured another bowlful of barley into the hole in the top stone. The kernels slipped between the two stones and were crushed into flour, enough for the *bet* with some left over for themselves.

Yana moved to the other side where the flour dribbled out of a hole in the bottom stone. She scooped a bowl of the fine powder and mixed it with water. As she'd done every day for as long as she could remember, she began making flatbread. To nourish all those at the bet, they would need over one hundred portions.

Marta soon joined them and began placing the formed rounds into the oven. Between the three of them, they finished all the bread they would need for the day before the sun was halfway to its height. Marta stacked them in a pair of large, flat baskets and covered them with a soft brown cloth made from an old tunic.

A round of hot bread held between her teeth, Miriam placed a pile of clean tunics in Yana's outstretched arms and picked up a smaller load herself, tucking it under one arm. She balanced one of the baskets against her other hip.

"Oh, wait. I forgot the oil." Marta set her basket on a low table nearby and rushed inside, reappearing almost instantly, a clay jar in her hand. "Now we can go." She chuckled softly. "I forget something nearly every day."

The trio strolled down the road until they reached the bet. The large house, larger even than Simeon's, sat back off the road to the west, nestled among towering date palms. They turned down the narrow dirt path that led to the entry of the enclosed courtyard.

Marta shoved the gate open with her knee and stepped into a large open area. A plot of vegetables occupied most of the left half, and several men knelt or even sat as they pulled up weeds. Women sat on the opposite side, spinning yarn from sheep's wool or weaving on looms leaning against the courtyard wall.

One of the women rose to greet them. "Good morning, girls."

Marta met her. "Hannah, I see you are up and outside. You must be feeling much better."

Hannah beamed. "I am. I hope to return home soon."

"Praise be to Adonai!"

"Yes. He has smiled on me."

Miriam and Yana left Marta handing out warm bread in the courtyard and walked through a narrow doorway on the left of the house that opened into a single open room for the women. Another door stood to the right, leading to a smaller room for men. Far more women came to be cared for than men.

They placed about two thirds of the tunics and the bread on a low table against the wall. Miriam took the remainder back outside for one of the men to take to the other side of the house, and Yana scanned the tired faces of the women lying on mats in orderly rows. Though her heart ached, she kept a smile on her face. These were some of Jerusalem's least fortunate. Deprived of any means to support themselves or ravaged by ill health and without anyone to care for—or even about—them, they had been dismissed to Bethany.

Alone. Destitute.

From a clay pitcher, Yana poured water into a dish. She grabbed two cloths from a shelf and knelt next to a young woman who had only recently come to the bet.

"Rada, how are you feeling today? You look a little stronger." Yana wet a cloth with the cool water.

Rada smiled weakly as she struggled to sit up. "I do feel a little better. It's the good food you give us here."

Yana placed a hand on her back and pushed her forward. "Soon you'll be on your feet, just like Hannah." Yana gently drew the damp cloth over Rada's flushed skin, wiping away hot sweat and grime.

Rada huffed, her eyes focused on the floor. "And then what? My husband divorced me when I got sick. I have nowhere to go. No way to live unless I sell myself."

"Nonsense. You can stay here. No one will be selling anything."

"Even when I am no longer ill?"

Yana pulled Rada's face toward hers. "Even then. You can help take care of those who are. That is what the bet is for. As long as there is Bethany, you will have a home. That, I promise you."

With the sun peering down into their courtyard from its highest point, Yana returned home to help Imma begin the evening meal. She drizzled some olive oil into a large pot and hung it over the firepit outside their house. After selecting some wild leeks and an onion, she chopped them into chunks while Imma minced a bulb of garlic. When they sprinkled the cut vegetables into the hot oil, the pungent fragrance quickly filled the courtyard.

As the vegetables and oil sizzled, Yana placed several handfuls of lentils and a splash of barley into the pot and then covered them with water. By tonight, the flavors would meld together to create a delicious evening stew.

Soon Yana would be doing all the cooking. "How do you make the stew taste so good?" she asked Imma. "Yours is always better than mine."

Imma laughed. "Your spices are not in balance. With some, you are too stingy, and with others, too free. And there are some that should not be added until the last hour." She patted Yana's hand. "Don't worry. I'll show you." She reached for a small jar. "Cumin is the most important." Imma filled her palm with the ground brown seeds and tossed them into the stew. "Not quite as much hyssop, and then only half that of sumac." She stirred the spices into the liquid. "We'll add coriander leaves at the end."

Yana shook her head. "I hope I can remember that. The cumin isn't very fragrant so I always add more."

"And far too much sumac. The scent of cumin isn't strong, but the flavor it delivers is." Imma chuckled. "We have a long while to practice."

With the stew gently warming, Imma climbed to the roof to rest.

Yana crossed the courtyard and tapped gently on the doorframe. "Uncle Simeon?"

He didn't turn around.

She knocked harder. "Uncle Simeon?"

He twisted from the waist and smiled brightly when his gaze caught hers. "*Motek*, I didn't hear you."

His term of endearment drew a smile from her lips. He was the only one who still called her *sweetheart*. She realized she hadn't smiled since he delivered his devastating news.

Simeon's house was bigger than any other in the village, but he used it all to help others. He made the large grain mill and the donkey that pulled it every morning available to all, after the bet's flour was ready. He offered shelter to those visiting families who had no extra room. Village meetings were held in their courtyard or in his common room when the weather wasn't cooperating. His wisdom and generosity made him a perfect leader.

"Is Ezi here?"

He shook his head slowly. "No, motek. He took the flocks back to the hills."

"Again? But why? He just got back."

"I think he needed time to think. To pray. He's as devastated as you are."

Her nose stung, and she sniffled. "I know he is."

Simeon neared her and wrapped an arm around her shoulders. "Come, sit with me." He led her to a stone bench covered with cushions.

Yana looked to him, silently pleading. "Is there anything we can do? Any way to stop this?"

"He is your abba—legally. His word is law. No one can overrule him, not even your imma. She can talk to him, but she cannot decree otherwise."

"You can't talk to him either?"

"I have no say whatsoever. I did try to talk to him, and I told him how much you and Eleazar mean to each other—have always meant to each other. It did no good."

"But how does this help him? What does he get from this match?"

"I don't know. I only know the man is very wealthy, very influential. Perhaps Lemuel thinks a connection with him will help him sell his wine."

Yana jumped up and stomped away, hands curled into fists. "This is so unfair! Why should I not have any say at all in how the rest of my life is to go?"

Simeon remained calm. "He should have consulted you, yes, but as you know, he doesn't have to abide by your wishes."

She huffed and crossed her arms over her chest. "He has never cared about me. Or Imma, as far as I can tell."

"When he first married her, he was devoted. He was good to her, and to you. He did everything he could to give her a good life, a better life. But he became obsessed with improving their status. Now that's all he cares about." Simeon rose and neared her again. "You know, life doesn't always go the way we plan it. I did not plan to lose my dear wife. Marta did not intend to lose her husband. All we can do is trust Adonai to work things out."

"But that's not the same! No one can stop death. But this—this is different. I should have a choice. I should be able to stop this before it starts."

"I realize women do not have the freedom men do. Perhaps that's not the way Adonai planned it from the beginning, but it is the way it is, and no amount of pouting, pleading, or wishing will change that."

"I can't change anything because I am nothing. No one cares what happens to me." She sounded like a spoiled child even to herself, but at the moment the pain was too great for her to worry about censoring her words.

Simeon gently grasped her shoulders. "Adonai cares for you."

"That's hard to believe right now," she whispered.

"I know. But you must trust in His goodness. Do you know what the prophet Zephaniah said about how much Adonai cares for us?"

She shook her head. She knew very little of the law and the prophets. She didn't even recognize the name. It was forbidden to formally teach the Torah to women, but Simeon had shared with her, as with his daughters, many of the sayings of the ancients.

"He said, 'The LORD your God is with you, the Mighty Warrior who saves. He will take great delight in you; in his love he will no longer rebuke you, but will rejoice over you with singing.' Think about that. Think about Adonai Himself rejoicing over you. He is the Creator, and He delights in you, His creation."

"I'll try."

He slid his arms around her back and hugged her.

Though he had no power to change anything, at least Simeon understood.

CHAPTER THREE

*This is what the L*ORD *says: "Let not the wise boast of their wisdom or the strong boast of their strength or the rich boast of their riches.*
~ Jeremiah 9:23 ~

Month of Av
Midsummer, AD 30
Bethany, Judea

The only people who came to Bethany were relatives of residents or Galileans on their way to or from Jerusalem. Occasionally, travelers too ill to continue on their journey between the Holy City and Jericho were forced to stop for a night or two to rest before they went on their way.

Generations ago, families from the fishing villages to the north settled here. Yana would never understand why, as Judeans as a whole looked down on those from Galilee. Their accented speech was viewed as sloppy, lazy. They were considered unsophisticated, too open to Greek influence, and too lax in their observation of the law. Anyone who needed a place to stay during the feasts, when Jerusalem was overfull, avoided the hospitality of Bethany, opting to stay in nearby Bethphage.

Unless they were Galileans as well.

So when a visibly prosperous merchant—and his donkeys and servants—turned off the Jericho road and headed toward their little village, word spread like a brush fire on the Mount.

Yana looked up from the tunic she was mending for the bet as a gaggle of boys raced down Bethany's only street, skipping and jumping until they reached the courtyard and ran toward Simeon. "A rich man is coming! A rich man is coming!"

"Thank you, boys." He ruffled their hair and moved toward her house. "He's here, Lemuel."

Yana started, jabbing the sharp needle into her finger. She wasn't expecting him to come so soon. His arrival meant betrothal, which meant no way out. Though she knew her future was decided, she'd harbored a flicker of hope something might yet stop it.

That hope fluttered out like a flame in a wind.

She put her finger in her mouth to stop the blood and hurried to the low wall surrounding their courtyard. Leaning on one palm, she searched the road, hoping to catch a glimpse of the man she'd been sentenced to spend the rest of her life with.

Simeon drew up behind her. "Inside, Yana, please. Let Lemuel greet him. If Oded wants to meet you, they'll let you know." He gently pulled her from the wall and turned her toward her house.

Of course. Why should she be included? It was only her life, after all.

"I'm sorry, motek." Simeon offered a sad smile and patted her shoulder.

Yana slipped inside as her imma hurried past her with arms full of baskets of fresh bread, early grapes, and dates. She placed them on the long, low table under a tree.

Pitchers of Lemuel's honeyed wine waited on a shelf in the broadroom. Yana grabbed two of them, along with the stack of clay cups, and carried them outside, ducking back inside just as Oded came into view. Two servants, each leading a donkey loaded with boxes and bags, followed close behind him.

Her stepfather brushed by her, hurrying to meet the spice dealer. "Oded, shalom." He embraced the man, kissing his cheek.

"Lemuel! Shalom. All is well."

Yana didn't have to strain to listen. His booming voice must have carried to the other end of the village.

Peering around the doorframe, she studied the man. He was not unhandsome but older than she had expected. Tall but stocky, he still had a full head of curly dark hair and a close-trimmed beard, both groomed with oil. His bleached white, ankle-length tunic was covered by a deep red robe, extensively embroidered with gold thread.

"I've brought gifts." Oded gestured to the shorter of the two servants, who grabbed bags from one of the donkeys and handed them to the other. The tall one, Greek in appearance, unwrapped each one before handing it to Oded.

"For your beautiful wife, some excellent olive oil, first press, and some freshly made wheat bread." He sniffed it. "Still warm." He grinned. "Ah. And this." He presented Imma with a wooden box about the size of both hands.

Imma set the oil and basket of bread at her feet to accept the gift. She lifted the lid with one hand, then brought the container to her face and inhaled. "Oh my...this is saffron." She raised her gaze to his face. "But this must have cost..." She smelled it again and nodded, erasing the awe from her face. "It smells wonderful. Thank you."

"You're very welcome. And for you, my cousin, spiced wine. Cinnamon, my favorite." He held out his offering. "One for today and one for you to keep."

He obviously preferred the most expensive of everything.

Behind his back, Lemuel closed one hand into a fist as he accepted the wine with the other. Oded's dismissal of Lemuel's wine would not sit well with him.

Yana trudged to the ladder at the back of the house and climbed to the roof. She dragged her reed mat to the edge closest to the courtyard, then lay on her back. Her head hidden by the low wall that circled the roof, she listened to the conversation below her, chewing on her thumbnail.

Why would he be interested in her? He was educated, successful, and richer than everyone in Bethany put together, several times over. There must by any number of beautiful young women in Jerusalem who would be delighted to marry him. Daughters of priests and Levites, of other merchants, women familiar with the ways of the Holy City.

She was only a villager, common, not educated.

So why did he want her?

While Imma, Oded, and Lemuel sat in the shade of the almond tree and discussed the possibility of marriage, Yana paced on the roof, careful to stay where she could hear and see without being seen. The sun beat down on her shoulders without mercy. They'd been eating, drinking, and talking since midday and showed no signs of nearing an end. The sun crept on its path from one horizon to the other like a desert tortoise. When would this day be over?

Laughter sounded occasionally as they leaned near each other, whispering. Oded didn't seem at all interested in meeting her. Marriages had been arranged by parents for their children since the beginning of time. Their forefather Isaac sent a servant to another land to find a bride for Jacob, but even Rebekah didn't have to go back with him if she didn't want to. Her abba said they would need to ask her first, and ever since, it had been traditional to obtain the girl's consent.

Traditional but not required.

The sun slid behind the top of the Mount of Olives, streaking the sky with pink and purple. Oded stood, and his servants hurried to pack up his donkeys. They would need to move quickly to reach Jerusalem before the sun fully set.

Yana watched as they lumbered down the street, heading north. Once they were no longer visible, she hurried down the ladder.

Imma breezed into the house, platters and pitchers in hand. "What a lovely, generous man!"

Yana flashed an insincere smile. She had no way of knowing if he was lovely, generous, or cruel. She'd not yet spoken a single word to the man. "I'll get the rest, Imma."

She headed for the table, now dotted with sparrows who had swooped down from the branches above, attacking the bread crumbs. "Go!" She shooed at the birds until they retreated to the tree, their chirps hounding her. *Tzip, tzip, tzip.* Foolish birds. Didn't they know they might be captured and eaten if they got too close? They seemed to have as little control over their lives as she did, except they didn't even realize it.

Six chalkstone plates—three unused—and the same number of mugs sat on the table. Where did they come from? They weren't Imma's, and as far as Yana knew, they didn't belong to Marta. Oded? He must have brought them as gifts. She'd heard that priests and the wealthy in Jerusalem used stone instead of clay, as it couldn't become ritually unclean. She stacked the dishes and brought them to the broadroom.

Imma took the utensils from her, put the small amount of food that remained untouched onto one of the clean plates, and offered it to Yana. "You haven't eaten yet, have you?"

She shrugged. "I wasn't hungry. I was too nervous."

"Then eat now." Imma fixed her with a stare not unlike the ones she gave Yana when she was a child threatening to disobey.

Yana accepted it. She still had no desire to eat, but she picked up a bunch of grapes and plucked one from the vine. She thought of Oded stuffing handfuls of the purple orbs into his mouth. He ate as much as any two men she knew. She would be in the kitchen all day once she married him. "I have a lot to learn about cooking in the next year." She laughed weakly.

Imma turned, wincing. "Actually, you don't have a year."

"The wedding will be in the spring?" Nine months wouldn't be too bad. Spring weddings were almost as common as those in autumn.

Lemuel entered the house. "No. You have three months."

Yana's sharp gasp cut through the air like an iron blade.

Three months. How could Lemuel agree to a wait of only three months? Why didn't Imma say anything?

"But I—I thought it would be a—a year," she stammered as she set the plate aside.

He waved the objection away. "A year is usually the time needed for the groom to build his house and sometimes gather or earn the bridewealth. Oded already has a house, and he obviously has the mohar."

Of course. A prosperous merchant like him would have it all in hand.

"He has everything a wife would need or want," he continued. "You will be his second, after all."

"What?" Yana stepped back as if she'd been punched, clutching her belly.

"He's *married*?" Imma's face revealed that this fact had been kept from her as well. She neared Yana and placed her hand softly on Yana's arm.

It was unusual but not against the law for a man to take a second wife. Only the wealthiest could afford two women, so if anyone could, it would be Oded.

"No!" Lemuel seemed shocked that they would think that of him, but Yana had no trouble believing it.

He shook his head violently. "I would never do that. You will be his only wife."

Yana sniffed. "He's a widower?"

"Apparently."

Yana picked at her nails. "But three months? Couldn't it be a little longer?"

"He wanted to marry you immediately. You should be thanking me that I managed to convince him to wait until after the Feast of Tabernacles. The cooler nights will be here then. The harvest will be over, and we'll have more for the wedding feast. Everything will be perfect."

No, it wouldn't.

Perfect would be marrying Ezi and staying in Bethany.

CHAPTER FOUR

He who finds a wife finds what is good
and receives favor from the LORD.
~ Proverbs 18:22 ~

Month of Elul
Late Summer, AD 30
Bethany, Judea

As it had been since time immemorial, men made all the decisions—when she would marry, whom she would marry, even where she would live.

Chewing on her nails, once again Yana paced on the roof.

Outside, Lemuel and Oded discussed her future. Again. They'd agreed to the match already, but this time the details would be decided: exactly when, where, and how much bride-wealth Oded would be required to give to her family.

Each had a bowl of Imma's sumptuous barley stew. Between them lay a platter of goat cheese, Oded's wheat bread, and a large bunch of Lemuel's grapes. Oded had again brought his own wine.

She heard laughing and the rustling of cloaks and dared to look over the roof's low wall. Lemuel whispered to Imma, who had just refilled their cups, and she moved toward the house. The men rose to their feet, Oded smiling broadly. They must have reached some arrangement agreeable to them both.

Just not to her.

"They want you to come down," said Imma, her head barely poking above the roof floor before she descended again.

Help me, Adonai. Yana smoothed her tunic, adjusted her head scarf and took a deep breath before crossing to the ladder and climbing down. Imma waited at the bottom.

"Must I do this?" She wrapped her arms around Imma's neck, desperately seeking a reprieve or at least comfort.

Imma patted her back. "Yes. You should be glad. I didn't meet your abba until the wedding."

That wasn't what she meant, but it was easy to see how Imma had misunderstood.

"I believe your groom has gifts for you." Imma grinned like a child who'd been promised a second honey cake.

Yana forced herself to step into the bright sunlight of the courtyard. She glanced across it to see Miriam hovering in her doorway, a bright smile lighting up her face.

Imma nudged her from behind, steering her toward her betrothed.

Oded approached, with a wide smile that didn't quite reach his eyes. He let his gaze drift over her, causing her to flinch as his eyes stayed a little too long in certain places. "Yana, I'm so glad to meet you. You are truly as beautiful as your abba claimed."

Is that why he wanted her? For beauty? She'd never thought of herself as beautiful. Ezi always said she was, but he loved her.

Imma had never told her that and certainly not Lemuel, nor had anyone else.

"I've brought you something." Oded bent and rummaged through a large pack at his feet, finally pulling out a tall, thin glass bottle about the size of a leek. "Lemuel may have told you that I'm a dealer of spices." His chest puffed out. "I supply many of the substances needed to make the temple incense. This is a perfume one of my shops creates." He stepped closer and pulled out the stopper. "What do you think?"

She sniffed. A delicate but intoxicating floral scent drifted up. "It's lovely. It smells like...a flower?"

"Jasmine." He grinned. "From Egypt. One more thing." He stooped to riffle through the bag once more.

Imma leaned near and placed her mouth next to Yana's ear. "I told you he was generous," she whispered.

Oded pulled out a tunic and held it up by the shoulders in front of her. "I believe this will fit perfectly. I had it made especially for you." He boasted like he had sewn it himself.

She blinked. Blue. The color of wedding clothes.

"Here. Take it." Oded shook it at her.

She reached for it.

How did he even know he and Lemuel would come to an agreement?

Let alone know this would fit her *perfectly*? He may be generous, but he was also incredibly presumptuous.

Now not only would men—a man—control where she lived and with whom, he would apparently also control what she wore.

But it had always been that way and would always be that way.

She might as well get used to it.

Month of Chesvan
Mid Fall, AD 30
Bethany, Judea

The three months since the betrothal had been finalized had gone quickly, and the wedding feast loomed over her like the rainy season's dark clouds.

The air had cooled considerably since midsummer. Jars of sun-dried raisins, spiced and honeyed wine, figs, and pomegranates, as well as the first of the olives lined the broadroom shelves next to spring's barley, chickpeas, and lentils. Except for the olives, which would continue to ripen until the middle of the rainy season, the harvest was completed. It had been plentiful, and everyone would have enough to last through the gray, rainy days of the wet season.

There would be plenty for a wedding feast as well. Lemuel was right—it would be perfect.

Or at least it would be if she had her own choice of husband.

Ezi had spent as much time as possible on the mountainside with the sheep. Away from Bethany. Away from her.

She needed to see him, needed to say goodbye before she left Bethany forever. She glanced at the sun hanging low in the west. Tomorrow was the Sabbath, and he almost always came home for Sabbath.

She headed north.

The last time she'd been here was the day Simeon told her she was to be betrothed. If only she could go back to that day, run away with Ezi before any of it happened.

Yana caught a glimpse of his tall, slender frame as he neared her.

He caught her glance, then abruptly turned back.

She ran after him. "Ezi?"

His shoulders tensed. His hands clenched into fists as he halted and slowly turned.

"Ezi, I'm sorry. Please don't be angry with me."

His eyes—bright, open eyes that had always held such light, such joy—widened. "Angry? Why would you think I'm angry with you?"

"You've avoided me ever since...since..."

He took a tentative step nearer. "Not because I'm angry." His voice was soft. He broke his gaze and looked over her shoulder. "I'm just trying to keep busy, so I don't have to think about..."

"Oh." She was grateful he wasn't angry, but in the end, it didn't really matter. She'd lost him months ago.

It was selfish, she knew, but she'd been counting on his strength. Until now, she hadn't truly realized how much this was hurting him. She'd only thought of her own pain. "What if we both just left?"

"What do you mean *left*?"

"Let's just go somewhere—somewhere that is not here. Some small village where no one knows us—and get married."

Ezi shook his head. "You always want to act before you think things through."

She crossed her arms. "What haven't I thought through?" He didn't need to treat her like a child.

"Say we do go somewhere. Where will we live? *How* will we live?"

"Then we'll go to a big city instead. We can go to Jericho or Sepphoris. Surely you can find someone who will hire you. You can work in a vineyard, or as a shepherd." She gestured toward the hills where he spent so much time with the flocks.

"Are you really willing to leave your family, to leave *my* family, and never see them again?" He held her gaze. "Do you really think this is what Adonai would want us to do?"

She squeezed her eyes shut. He was right. Of course he was right. And even if she didn't think he was, her beloved would never do anything so dishonorable.

"Should we say goodbye now then? Or will you be there?"

"I'm not sure I can do that. I feel like I'm dying already." Ezi squeezed his eyes tight and ran his hand down his beard. "How can I watch you be given to another?"

"I understand." She wouldn't be able to see him anyway. Men and women were separated. From the night before, through the entire next day of the festivities, she would be with the women, until she left with Oded at sunset for the marriage chamber.

The faintest hint of a smile graced his lips. "I have something for you. I was going to leave it with your imma, but now…" He slipped his hand into the bag over his shoulder that held his food and a supply of olive oil to tend to the wounds of the sheep. He withdrew a white jar and held it up for her. It was too big for his hand to wrap completely around, and about twice as tall. Sunlight hit the translucence, highlighting the fine graining.

She reached for it, ran her fingers over the smooth, white substance.

"It's alabaster," he said.

"It's beautiful."

"My abba gave this to my imma the day I was born. It holds spikenard oil, worth about a year's wages. I was always told it was mine to give to my betrothed."

The neck was long and slender, sealed. In order to use it, it would have to be broken.

Searing pain ripped through her heart.

She'd never seen, let alone held, anything so beautiful, so precious. But it meant nothing without him. She put her hand over his and shoved it back toward him. "Ezi, you have to keep this. There will be someone else, and you—"

"There will never be anyone else. I want you to have it. I've thought of giving you this for over a year." His voice broke. "Even if I… This could only belong to you." He clasped his hands around hers. "Please. Take it."

His hands were rough and warm, strong and gentle. She nodded as he pulled his hands away and clasped them behind his back.

"I'm leaving as soon as Sabbath is over. I'm going to Galilee to stay with Abba's relatives for a while."

They were her relatives too, her abba's cousins, though she hadn't seen them in years, since they left Galilee. Perhaps he hadn't thought of that.

She studied him, committing his face to memory. The scar on his chin from when he pretended to be a bird, jumped from the roof, and hit a rock. The freckles on his nose that gathered into one spot when he laughed. The lock of hair on the crown of his head that refused to lie flat no matter how long it grew.

He placed his hand on her cheek and bent toward her. The warmth of his touch sent a shiver though her. Just when she thought he would kiss her one last time, he placed a kiss on her cheek instead. "Goodbye, Eliyanah."

He trudged past her toward his home without looking back.

The ache in her chest grew stronger as she watched him grow smaller. Would she ever see him again?

CHAPTER FIVE

*If a man has recently married, he must not be
sent to war or have any other duty laid on him.
For one year he is to be free to stay at home and bring
happiness to the wife he has married.*

~ Deuteronomy 24:5 ~

Adonai had not answered her prayer.

On her back on the roof, arms under her head, Yana
stared at the dusky gray sky. If Adonai had granted her prayer,
the prayer she had whispered over and over until she drifted
off to sleep, the sun would not be lightening the sky at this very
moment. It would have stayed, hiding its face, refusing to shine
on this despised day.

She had vowed to do her best to make this marriage work,
but now that the day had arrived, she was finding it more
difficult—and painful—than she had anticipated.

Last night, while Oded dined with the men of the village,
the young women had swarmed around her, rubbing the indigo
cloth of her tunic between their palms, running their fingers
along the fine lines of the gold embroidery around her collar
and down her sleeves. They counted the silver coins of her
dowry sewn into her headdress and passed her sandals among

themselves, pointing out the jewels to one another and guessing the names. They repeatedly told her how very lucky she was that such a rich and successful man wanted her to be his wife. Any one of them would gladly trade places with her.

She would gladly let them.

Her ritual bath had been completed yesterday. All that remained was to rise, dress, and await the beginning of the feast.

She could say one more prayer, but why bother? Adonai wasn't listening to her.

Her heart heavy, she sat up. She looked out over the village she claimed as home. She had enjoyed her last night under Bethany's stars.

She climbed down the ladder and trudged outside. As he had promised, Lemuel had used part of the bridewealth to provide an elaborate wedding feast. He didn't want to be embarrassed.

Nor did he want to appear too common, too poor while Oded was here.

Imma had set out baskets of dates, figs, pistachios, and roasted barley kernels, along with jugs of spiced olive oil. Her friends Rachel and Elizabeth busily kneaded dough for bread, and Susannah and Elisheba boiled grape leaves, later to be stuffed with pine nuts, chopped dried fruit, and onions and garlic cooked in olive oil.

But what Imma and Lemuel had provided, impressive as it was, was nothing compared to what Oded had brought with him yesterday. The courtyard's two firepits were blazing. One spit held a lamb, the other held a calf. Hardly a breath could be taken without inhaling the tantalizing scents of spices, roasting flesh, and burning wood.

Marta and Miriam had spent the better part of yesterday grinding flour for bread from the wheat he'd brought, along with pomegranates and almonds, and most noticeably, the stone jars full of wine which now lined the edges of the courtyard.

Imma patted her shoulder. "Inside! This is not a time for you to help!" She chuckled. "Get dressed and rest. The day will be busy soon enough." Imma shooed her inside with one hand while beckoning with the other. "Marta!"

Marta hurried over and drew Yana inside. "Let's get your tunic on again." She retrieved the garment Yana had hung on a peg last night. "This is so beautiful. I wore my imma's tunic when I married."

"Did you know him?"

"My husband?"

"Yes, before you married him?"

"No. His family was new to our village, but they were Galileans. That helped. We had much in common."

"And did you love him?"

"Not at first. But I liked him, and we came to love each other very much." Her eyes misted.

"Oh, Marta, I'm so sorry. I didn't mean to bring up unhappy memories."

"No, it's all right. I miss talking about him. Nothing about my life with him was unhappy, until the end. Come now, let's get you dressed."

The gold thread glistened in the sunlight that crept through the small window. It was lovely, but Yana still chafed at wearing something Oded had picked out.

As soon as she stepped outside, she was surrounded by the village's young women. They would feast beside her and dance around her, exulting in her new life.

If only she shared that joy.

In moments the sun would slide behind the Mount of Olives.

Yana's stomach growled and she placed a hand over her belly in a vain attempt to quiet it. She'd only nibbled some soft wheat bread all day. She'd tried to make herself eat, but everything tasted like sand. Rich food, spiced wine, lively music, and dancing surrounded her, but she hardly noticed.

The dancing, feasting, and celebration would last all night, but she and Oded would retire to the wedding chamber to make the marriage finally complete. Legal and insoluble.

Imma knelt behind her. "It's time. He waits for you." She pointed a finger over Yana's shoulder at Oded, who waited just beyond the group of women, talking to Lemuel.

Yana drew in a long, shuddering breath. She rose and allowed Imma to lead her to her groom.

Oded nodded and silently turned toward the house across the courtyard.

She could do nothing but follow him.

Hazy morning light slowly drew Yana back to consciousness. She glanced around the room—not her house. Simeon's house. As a child, she'd often spent the night here with Miriam, but this morning, something was different. What?

Soft snoring beside her reminded her. She turned to see her new husband, his back to her, sound asleep.

Her *husband*. She was married.

Thoughts about the night before filled her mind. There had been no tenderness to him at all. He'd been rough and quick. Had he even kissed her once? When he was finished, he turned to face the wall and fell asleep without a word.

It had not been what she expected, what she'd heard whispered at the well. Yet she had also heard the first time was almost never pleasant. Perhaps it would get better as time went on and they came to love each other.

Oded rolled onto his back and blinked. Silently, he rose, slipped on his linen tunic, and left the room.

He must have gone outside to relieve himself. They were to remain in the bridal chamber, alone, for seven days. This was a time not only to consummate their union but to get to know each other.

After all, she'd spoken only a few sentences to him.

While he was out, she pulled out one of the tunics he had brought for her. Dyed with weld, it was a beautiful bright yellow.

She slipped it on. The fabric was just as supple as the wedding garment. Nothing like the coarse wool she was used to. She'd expected to wear clothing so expensive only once in her life. She sifted through the other tunics. All were as soft as flower petals.

She paced while she waited, fear and anticipation mingling.

When he didn't return, she opened the door that led to the common area.

Oded sat cross-legged on a cushion at the low stone table, parchments spread across the table. The servant who had come with him—the tall one—sat across from him, a wax tablet on his lap, busily marking as Oded read one parchment after another, barking out orders.

Business? How could he conduct business during their wedding week?

She gasped softly.

He whipped his head around. "You belong inside." He glared.

So do you.

She ducked back inside and dropped onto the bed.

Oded shoved open the door. "I leave on a very important buying trip next week, and I need to make preparations."

"Oh," she whispered. "All right. How long will you be gone?"

"Until my business is completed." He turned and left, closing the door behind him.

How often did he travel? How often would she be left alone?

For the third day, Oded had spent his time with his servant discussing his upcoming trip. She and Oded had not shared a meal together, had a conversation, or spent any time together whatsoever.

At night, after he completed his husbandly duty, noiselessly and with little evidence of any enjoyment, he rolled over and fell asleep. He arose and left her before she awakened.

Yana felt like one of Jacob's sheep, of value only to produce the spotted or streaked lambs their forefather had desired.

She slipped out of the room and padded into the broad-room of Simeon's house. No use staying in their room all day yet again. She was not used to being idle, so she might as well accomplish something today. But what? Marta and Miriam delivered their food, the house needed no cleaning, and she couldn't very well leave for the bet.

She found a pair of looms standing against the wall. They probably hadn't been worked since before the fall harvest began. The hard work of storing enough food for the rainy season claimed all of everyone's time. Weaving was left for the long, dreary days of winter, when the wheat and barley were left for Adonai to tend.

One loom was nearly full of deep red and indigo blue yarn in an intricate pattern. *Must be Miriam's.* Marta was nowhere near patient, or imaginative, enough to create such a beautiful piece of cloth. She would see it as a waste of precious time. Marta had to be working on the other one. Irregular stripes the creamy natural color of sheep's wool and smaller stripes of the less common black and a lighter tan filled about half of the loom. In several places, she had either skipped a yarn or taken two at a time. Marta much preferred cooking.

Yana turned to face the expansive shelves behind her. Baskets and jars were crammed in every available space. Searching until she found baskets of yarn, she then retrieved the darkest brown and sat at the bottom of Marta's loom. She pulled on the weights hanging near the floor to straighten out the lax strands, then began weaving the dark yarn over and under the lighter yarn that stretched from top to bottom.

After she'd woven several rows, she looked up at the other rows of the same wool, deciding whether it was time to change colors.

She tensed at the sound of heavy footsteps outside the room. Would Oded be angry she'd left their room? How could he when he was never in it himself?

He poked his head in. "There you are."

She froze, awaiting a scolding.

"We'll leave after the midday meal. I must go to Petra." He left without further explanation.

After only three days? Wedding feasts never lasted less than five, and often lasted a full week. She would never have imagined hers would be less than four.

Then again, since the day she knew she'd been betrothed, nothing had been as she imagined.

Yana and Imma stood by the donkey as Oded and his servant—Alexander?—loaded it for the journey to Jerusalem.

The journey *home*. Would she ever think of it as truly home?

Imma hugged her. "I'm so happy for you. I know he will provide wonderfully for you. You will lack nothing."

Only the most important things. Love. Bethany. You. Ezi. She shook her head to stop the traitorous thoughts.

Simeon approached. "Goodbye, motek. We will miss you." He pulled her near and embraced her. "Listen for Him singing over you," he whispered.

She nodded. "I'll try."

She wasn't sure how, but she was certain that if Adonai loved her as Simeon said, He would help her be a good wife to this man she barely knew. He would allow her to hear Him singing.

Though she couldn't imagine how, she'd never wanted anything more.

CHAPTER SIX

Just as the rich rule the poor, so the borrower is servant to the lender.
~ Proverbs 22:7 ~

Yana had made the short journey to Jerusalem only once before, and she'd been too young then for her to remember any of the mountainous climb now.

Women were not required to attend the feasts in Jerusalem, so they remained behind, cooking and taking care of the myriad of guests that flooded Bethany three times a year.

Massive, gnarled olive trees lined the dirt road on either side as if guarding the ancient path, with an occasional fig or acacia tree thrown in. Thornbushes boasted bloodred flowers, and blue hyacinths stretched their necks to the sky, soaking in the last of the sun before the rainy season hit. Butterflies and bees chased each other among the blossoms in an intricate dance.

But the cheerful landscape belied Yana's dark mood. They were three-quarters of the way there, and Oded had yet to speak to her. Or even look at her.

Or acknowledge her at all.

Had she really expected anything different? Certainly not after this week, which should have been the happiest of her life.

Oded walked far ahead, his servant behind him leading the loaded donkey. The clothes Oded had brought filled one bag. He'd worn a different robe each day over his bleached tunic. At least he'd traded his jeweled sandals for a simpler pair for the long walk. The new tunics he'd brought for her were in a second bag. Items relating to his business filled a third. Several empty bags—the ones that had been filled with gifts— were draped over a second donkey plodding obediently behind the first.

She'd tucked the alabaster jar among her dowry coins in a small bag she carried. Oded had told her to bring nothing— that everything she'd need would be waiting.

How could he possibly know what she needed?

Then again, the blue-trimmed tunic he'd brought had fit her perfectly. As did the sandals.

At first she believed, or at least wanted to, that his careful observance was due to kindness. Due to a sincere desire to do whatever he could to make her happy.

That was when she still had hope. When she tried to believe that Oded could make her as happy as Ezi would have. Over the last four days that hope had been shattered, like an oil lamp thrown to the ground, the light flickering and disappearing forever.

All the fine clothing did nothing to soothe her injured heart now.

She continued trudging up the hill, sweat dripping down her back. If they'd left at dawn, the sun wouldn't be beating down on her shoulders, but Oded had chosen to leave at the most uncomfortable part of the day. Even with the rainy season on the horizon, the sunshine in the open air could be brutal. Hot, unmoving dry air hovered over them, and she coughed as dust coated her face and throat.

A pebble kicked up by one of Oded's donkeys lodged in her sandal. The pain shot through the thin leather and she stumbled. She shook her foot in a vain attempt to dislodge the rock, then stopped and reached down to remove her sandal and release the stone trapped between the sole and her bare foot. She rubbed the tender skin. A bruise would surely form. She laid her sandal on the dirt road and slipped her foot into it, taking in the landscape around her. The soft call of sheep mingled with the bleating of goats.

Was Ezi nearby, leading the flock to the greener grass atop the mountain?

Fingering the jar stashed in her bag, she searched for him, throwing glances at Oded to make sure he didn't notice what she did. Finally, in the distance and slightly above where she now stood, she saw Ezi, calmly walking ahead of the animals, calling to them, encouraging them to follow.

Why would he be here today? He should have known she would be going to Jerusalem—to her new home—this morning. Why would he risk bumping into her with her new husband?

The answer jolted her like the pebble in her sandal. Oded had made them leave three days early. Ezi would have thought today safe.

Her heart broke again. Why did she have to marry this man who could barely remember her name, when she wanted

Ezi? Ezi, who was unfailingly kind and gentle, who wanted to be her husband as much as she wanted to be his wife.

She shook her head. Thoughts like that would do her no good. Her future had been decided, and she needed to do whatever she could to make the best of it.

She caught up with Oded at the crest of the Mount of Olives. Her eyes followed the winding path down the mountain to the bottom of the valley, then back up. She gasped as she beheld the Holy City she'd heard about from so many travelers.

A wide, gray stone wall circled the city. The first walls had been destroyed by the Babylonians over five hundred years ago, but the king of Persia allowed Nehemiah to return to Jerusalem and rebuild them. At intervals along the wall were wide gateways and soaring towers. The Temple Mount nestled up to the walls on the eastern side of the city. The white and gold of the temple itself, dwelling place of Adonai on earth, gleamed brighter than the sun.

Small limestone houses were packed beside narrow, unpaved streets that sloped southward from the mount. Across the Tyropean Valley, which ran north to south through the center of Jerusalem, white marble villas and palaces sprawled, demanding notice. A large bridgeway supported by enormous arches spanned the valley, crossing from these houses over the valley to the temple.

Yana realized that Oded had marched on without her, and she struggled to keep up yet still maintain her balance on the steep path downhill. At the bottom of the valley they turned toward the southernmost gate. They passed under the arch, the Pool of Siloam to their right.

The road, crafted of enormous wide stones, rose toward the temple. Every so often, a short series of steps eased the climb. Small shops, shaded by large cloths attached to the mud-brick walls on either side, lined the dusty street. A baker removed bread from an oven built into the ground. A tailor busily stitched cloth with a bronze needle. Perfume bottles and jewelry were crowded onto tables. Most merchants were men but a few women sold dyed wool or yarn, and others hawked rugs and other woven items.

As they moved north, the shops grew larger and were made of stone. They were tucked under the staircase that rose from the market street to the southwest corner of the temple. Food replaced pottery and clothing. Everything from fresh fruits and vegetables to dried fish was proudly displayed. The smells of sweaty bodies, dried fish, and fresh bread filled her nose while the clanging of metal, shouting of vendors, and cries of small children rang in her ears, and the crowd pressing in on her threatened to steal her breath.

She craned her neck to catch a glimpse of the temple rising above its protective walls.

It was said Solomon's temple, destroyed along with the walls by Nebuchadnezzar, was even more ornate and majestic. But how could anything be more impressive than this one? Golden pyramids around the top of the walls were topped by gold spikes to keep ravens away. Wisps of smoke rose to heaven, allowing a sweet smell to linger. Sunlight bounced off white marble and golden gates.

Oded turned left under the bridge and climbed a gently rising street. As they trod the narrow alleyways between two-story houses, the chaos of the market fell away.

Yana smiled politely as Oded boasted.

"This is cedar, imported from Lebanon. You will notice very few houses with such a luxury." He drew his fingers over the wide double door. "I had these grapevines carved into the wood. It took three craftsmen more than a week to complete it."

A needless proclamation of the lavishness that apparently awaited within. Trees were few in Judea and rarely were any of the trunks thick enough to be cut and used for building materials. Only the extraordinarily wealthy could afford Lebanon's cedar. And two doors when one was more than wide enough was nothing more than pride.

Until now, the biggest house Yana had ever seen was Simeon's, and it appeared, from the outside at least, that four houses that size would fit inside this one—and there would still be room.

Oded opened the door and moved aside to let her pass. "Come in, come in."

Yana stepped through the outer gate into an enormous, tiled, open-air courtyard. A row of columns separated this area from a room beyond, and more rooms lined either side. A pool of water with a small fountain occupied the center. Slowing as she passed it, she placed her hand under the flow of cool water spouting up from the center. She wiggled her fingers, sending droplets in every direction.

A young female servant appeared to greet them and bowed to her. "Please sit, so I may wash your feet."

Yana drew back. Only her imma had ever washed her feet, and that was when she was a child. No one in Bethany had servants, so people took care of their own needs. She washed the feet of those in the bet; people didn't wash hers.

The servant gestured to the seat next to the door.

Yana backed up to the white stone stool and sat. A silver pitcher, bowl, and towel waited on a pedestal beside her.

The girl reached for the bowl and placed it next to the stool. She looked a year or two younger than Yana, light brown hair pulled into a long braid. Full lips, gray-blue eyes. She wore a simple tunic and her feet were bare.

She picked up one of Yana's feet and removed her sandal. She poured water from the pitcher over her foot, washing away the dust of the journey, then dried it off. She repeated the ritual with the other foot.

"Thank you," Yana whispered.

When Yana did not rise, the servant leaned toward her as she rose to replace the pitcher. "Now you offer to wash the *ba'al's* feet." She tipped her head toward Oded. "It is improper for any woman but his wife to do so."

Yana's mouth formed an O. She rose and crossed the room to stand before Oded. "May I wash your feet, *Ba'ali*?"

Oded blinked, as if he had not yet noticed her standing there. He nodded and sat.

Yana reached for the bowl and pitcher by the stool and did exactly as the servant had done for her. As she dried his feet, sandaled footsteps sounded behind her.

"Welcome home, brother."

Oded rose to embrace his brother. "Thank you, Elon. It's good to be home."

Still kneeling at her husband's feet, Yana stole a glance at Elon. He looked very much like Oded, same build, same height, softer eyes.

"How was your trip to the village?" Elon looked down at her. "This is the girl?"

"Yes." Oded wrapped an arm around his brother's shoulders. "We need to talk about Petra." They walked away, toward the only door on the left, and disappeared behind it.

What did she do now? Should she just try to find their room? She was supposedly the *ba'alah* of the house now, but she had no idea where anything was. And from how Oded had acted so far, the last thing she wanted to do was anger him.

Another young servant, with a kind face and a wide smile, approached her.

"Shalom. You must be Oded's new wife. I'm Diana." She reached for the dusty bundle Yana had carried from Bethany. "I clean the ba'al's house and clothes. Let me show you to your room."

Diana led her to the right, toward the corner in the back of the house. As they approached a staircase, Yana peeked in the room closest to it.

She gasped. A *mikveh*. A ritual bath *inside the house*.

She followed Diana up the wide steps. Not even Simeon had a stone staircase.

At the top, a narrow hallway stretched from the staircase to the opposite wall, then turned left to run alongside the south side of the house. An iron railing instead of a wall on the outer edge allowed a view of the room below as well as the Temple Mount.

Diana led her down the hallway and entered the room in the southwest corner.

Yana gingerly took one step forward, halting just inside the spacious chamber.

Diana swept a hand across the room. "This will be your sleeping chamber. It should already have everything you need, but if you find there is anything you lack, I'll be happy to help you."

A wooden bed with a luxurious soft blue covering over a thick mattress stood against the middle of the far wall. It was wide enough for only one person.

Yana felt like she'd been punched in the gut. "I don't share a room with Oded?"

"This is where his first wife stayed. But everything in here has been replaced. There is nothing remaining of hers."

Why would that be important? Then a thought hit her. "She didn't—she didn't die in here, did she?"

Diana frowned, her face revealing her horror at the thought. "No, of course not." She turned—apparently the conversation was closed—and crossed to a corner of the room, where a stone three-legged table sat below a highly polished bronze mirror.

She picked up a small jar, removed the top, and sniffed, then offered it to Yana.

"Jasmine?"

She smiled. "Yes. You know your perfume."

Yana shook her head. "I don't know much at all about it."

"You will learn, whether you want to or not." She replaced the bottle. "There is an assortment of lotions and perfumes. If there is anything missing, or even if you would simply prefer another scent, please let me know." She moved to a trunk at the foot of the bed, lifted the lid, and pulled out an embroidered tunic. She held it up to Yana and flashed a bright smile. "It seems these will fit you."

Yana fingered the soft fabric. The design was stitched in multiple colors. It must have been incredibly expensive. She stepped closer to the trunk. Stacks of vibrantly colored garments filled the box almost to overflowing. "No wonder he said I didn't need to bring anything."

Diana chuckled dryly. "No, I'm sure he said he would provide everything you could possibly need, and he will. He is a very generous man."

An older woman appeared in the open door, a platter filled with grapes, figs, and warm bread in her hands.

Diana nodded to her. "Please come." She closed the lid of the chest and pointed to it. "Thank you."

"I'll return with wine." The woman placed the platter on the trunk and slipped out.

"That was Sopha. She prepares all the food. Her husband, Kronos, takes care of the house."

Yana slowly turned around, examining the room and all its furnishings. Another table sat in the opposite corner, with a jeweled box sitting atop it. Yana lifted the lid and gasped. Inside were necklaces, bracelets, earrings…and not made of beads but of gold and jewels.

"I'm sure you're exhausted from your trip." Diana glanced around the room again. "I'll let you get settled, and I'll come get you when it's time for the evening meal." She reached for the door.

"Diana?"

"Yes, Ba'alah?"

Yana cringed at the title. "Please don't call me that."

Diana looked confused. "We have been instructed to. The ba'al would be angry."

"When we're alone then? Please call me Yana."

"As you wish."

Yana turned back to the chest and gestured to it. "How did he know they would fit me?"

"I'm not sure, but after he returned from Bethany the first time, he had all of these made for you."

Yana felt like she'd been slapped. "I hadn't even agreed to marry him then."

Diana's face darkened. "Somehow, the ba'al always gets what he wants."

CHAPTER SEVEN

*It is better to live in a desert land than with a contentious
and vexing woman.*
~ Proverbs 21:19 ~

Yana lowered herself to the bed and sank deep into the
mattress. She leaned over, pulled up the covering, and
poked at the mattress. The outside was remarkably soft. It
wasn't wool—perhaps fine linen?—and it wasn't stuffed with
straw. Maybe stuffed with wool? She replaced the covering and
slid her hand over the fabric fit for a king. She'd heard of silk.
Was this what it felt like?

She slipped the bag from her shoulder and placed it gently
in the middle of the bed. Picking it up by the bottom corners,
she allowed the contents to slide out.

Her dowry and Ezi's jar of nard. What to do with them?
Hide them?

Surely Oded would not be happy if he knew she'd kept
Ezi's gift. But the dowry—he could have that any time he liked.

Stuffing the silver pieces back in the bag, she scanned the
room. Her eyes landed on the trunk at the foot of her bed.
They'd be safe there, not on display but not so out of sight he
could accuse her of trying to keep them from him. She lifted

the lid and placed the bag at the bottom under all the tunics, then spread them back out and shut the lid.

Now the jar. That she did want to hide, and hide well. But the only thing that closed in any way was the trunk. She sat again on the bed, leaning back on her hands, trying to think of some way to conceal the gift.

What about the mattress?

She dropped to the floor and shoved the covering away. A seam ran around three sides, keeping the wool in its place. If she placed the jar deep in the wool and sewed it up again, no one would ever find it.

She moved to the head of the bed and ran her fingers along the seam. She grabbed at a thread and broke it, then unwound it from the cloth until she had a hole large enough for the jar. She jammed it inside, making sure enough wool surrounded it on all sides so it could not be seen or felt from the outside.

All she needed now was a needle to keep her secret safe.

As the sun slipped closer to the horizon, Yana opened the door to her chamber and peered out. The upper floor had three rooms along the back wall, and another, much larger one, was next to hers on the south. The northern side had only one apparently very large room. The house was shaped much like her simple stone home in Bethany but in every other way was shockingly different. She descended the stairs and stepped into the courtyard filled with golden sunlight. Long shadows stretched across the stone floor.

Yana moved to the fountain. Water spit high into the air then collapsed again into the pool, only to be tossed toward the sky again. In Bethany, water was precious. Women trekked to the center of the village each morning to lower their buckets into the darkness of the well, then haul them back up full of water and many times heavier. Their mikveh was the small river nearby where they also washed clothes. No one would consider wasting water in a fountain, even if it was beautiful and produced a calming and soothing sound.

A young woman approached. She was about Yana's age and wore a deep blue robe with a headscarf in a softer shade. Her eyes were ringed with black, and her lips and cheeks were tinged with pink. "You must be Eliyanah. I'm Basya."

She said it like Yana was supposed to know who she was. "Basya? Do you live here?"

She frowned. "Didn't Oded tell you about us?"

"Us?"

She sighed. "That's just like him." She put a hand to her chest, dipping her head slightly. "I am married to Oded's younger brother, Elon. We live here along with their mother, Naomi."

"Oh." No, Oded hadn't bothered to tell her about his family. She'd been led to believe he had none. None came to the wedding. "I didn't know anyone else lived here."

"Yes. Our sleeping chamber is in the corner opposite yours. Naomi's is between ours, and Oded's is the large one on the south wall."

Yana nodded, still trying to figure out why he had not mentioned his family. Or invited them to the wedding.

"There are also several servants," added Basya. "They sleep downstairs."

"Yes, I've heard them." Yana gestured toward the large room in the corner. "That must be them putting food on the table."

Basya glanced over her shoulder. "Oded calls that the *triclinium*. It's a Latin word. He's fascinated with Roman culture, as you can tell from the house."

"Tri...what?"

"It just means a room to eat in." She laughed. "We don't call it that, and you don't have to either."

"Do you call this room something else as well?"

"This is the atrium. Again, Latin."

"Can you tell me what this is for?" Yana wiggled her fingers in the water.

"Just decoration. It's magnificent, isn't it?"

"It seems like a waste of water."

Basya laughed. "You really are a simple girl, aren't you?"

Yana's ears burned. She'd never fit in here.

Basya reached for her forearm, eyes wide. "I didn't mean that how it sounded. I mean that you're uncomplicated. You say what you think, and you don't waste time trying to impress others. Half the people in Jerusalem lie half the time, whether it's necessary or not. And *everyone* wants more. More power, more things, more people to serve them, more respect."

Yana turned as footsteps at the bottom of the stairs drew their attention. An elegant older woman glided toward them.

Basya threaded her arm though the woman's. "Eliyanah, this is Naomi, Oded and Elon's imma."

The woman raised her chin, seeming to look down on Yana though she was the same height. "So you are my son's new wife."

"I am. Usually I am called Yana."

Naomi's eyes were hard, and she slowly moved her gaze down Yana from head to sandals, in much the same way as Oded had done when they first met.

Yana nearly shivered under her glare.

"Oded was right," said Naomi. "Your accent is atrocious. I told him not to marry a Galilean." She shrugged. "But what's done is done. You may as well join us for the evening meal."

Yana headed for the dining area in the corner on the other side of the columns, but Basya grabbed her hand. "Except for feast days, we eat in the women's room." She led Yana to the front of the house on the right side of the courtyard.

Naomi opened the door and entered, but Basya allowed Yana to precede her into the room. A tile mosaic covered most of the floor, leaving a border of shiny white marble all around. A small, low table, surrounded by cushions, occupied the far half of the room. Closer to them, a pair of Roman-style couches flanked a round stone table, with more cushions scattered around.

Naomi and Basya lowered themselves onto two of the cushions dyed a brilliant blue.

Diana appeared at Yana's elbow. "Would you like to sit?" She gestured toward the table.

Yana smiled. "May I help you with the meal at all first?"

Basya snickered.

Diana blushed a deep crimson. "No, of course not," she whispered. "Please sit. We will serve you."

Yana grimaced. The other two stared at her, Naomi with clear disdain. She pointed at a cushion, silently commanding Yana to sit.

She obeyed. "I didn't know Oded had a brother." Maybe she could steer the conversation away from her unworthiness.

Basya smiled. "Elon works with Oded. He often travels with him, so a great number of days it will be just the three of us."

And the servants.

Basya smiled. "I'm delighted to have a sister-in-law again."

Again. Yana had almost forgotten she was a second wife. "I'm very grateful I won't be alone so often. I didn't realize Oded would be traveling so much."

Sopha entered the room, placing platters of meat, hot bread, and fruit on the table.

"Is this a special occasion?" asked Yana.

Basya's brow furrowed. "No, why?"

"Well, the meat." She gestured to the platter heaping with sliced meat.

Naomi rolled her eyes. "We eat meat most days. Don't you?"

"No, of course not."

Naomi scoffed.

Everything she said seemed to disappoint Naomi.

Naomi beamed at Basya as she reached for a chunk of meat. "Basya has given me two grandsons."

"How wonderful. I can't wait to have a son."

Naomi nodded approvingly. "That will be an auspicious day indeed."

"Especially after what happened—"

"Basya, quiet!"

After what happened? "What do you mean?"

Basya stared at her hands, saying nothing.

Naomi glared at Basya, then, donning an insincere smile, turned to Yana. "It's nothing for you to worry about." She waved a hand. "In fact, you have nothing at all to be concerned about. There are servants to care for the house, to cook, to grind the grain for the bread—the only thing you need to attend to is producing at least one son. Obey your husband, give him a son, and you will lack for nothing."

The rest of the meal proceeded in awkward conversation about the coming rains, the food, anything but what Basya had alluded to.

After the meal Yana returned to her room. She lay on the bed and stared at the ceiling, Naomi's warning echoing in her mind.

"Obey your husband, give him a son, and you will lack for nothing."

What was that supposed to mean? It seemed to be an implied threat. And if she didn't give him a son? What would she end up *lacking*?

She didn't want to think about that.

Yana strolled in the atrium, still dumbfounded by the thought of water in the house. The tinkling sound of splashing liquid reminded her of the babble of the brook back home.

Oded had been gone for a week, and with nothing to clean or cook and no one to care for, she was at a loss.

She really needed to learn her way around this place.

Three doors broke up the long northern wall. The first, closest to the street, led to the women's room. She opened the middle door to find a storage room. Perfume bottles, acacia wood boxes, and alabaster jars—though not as large as hers—filled the shelves built into the wall. The third door, closest to the mikveh and staircase, contained nothing but a low bed with a mattress. Backing out, she nearly bumped into Basya. "Oh, I am so sorry!"

Basya only laughed. "Have you been to the market yet?"

"We passed through it when we arrived."

"No, no. That's the lower market. We shop at the market very near here, across from Herod's palace."

She spoke Herod's name as if he were a friend.

"Come with me. We'll get you some money from Alexander."

Why would Alexander give her money?

Behind Oded's workroom, next to the dining area, a slightly open door led to a room about half the size of the workspace.

Basya rapped on the door.

Yana heard shuffling, and Alexander came to greet them. His dark hair was cropped short and he was clean-shaven. He was younger than she'd thought from her brief glimpses of him. Taller than both of them, he smiled down on them. "Yes?"

Basya pushed Yana forward. "She needs some money. We're going to the market."

"Very well." He extended an arm, inviting them in.

The room was bigger than it looked to be from the atrium. A stuffed mattress on a low bed occupied the far corner. A wide table sat against the wall, covered with parchments, wax tablets, and tiny jars of ink.

"Oh, I forgot the yarn I need to match for tomorrow. I'll be right back." Basya hurried back to the stairs.

Alexander pulled a wooden box closer then retrieved a tiny silver key from around his neck and unlocked it.

"How much?" He looked at Yana, but she lifted her shoulders.

"I have no idea. I've never bought anything with coins." In Bethany they had everything they needed, and what they didn't have they traded for. When anyone left money for the village, whether passing through or after spending Pesach there, it went to Simeon, who used it to purchase needed supplies for the bet. The donkey-powered grain mill was one of his purchases, after saving for several years.

Alexander grinned. "What do you plan to buy?"

Could she feel any more stupid? She had no idea what they even had at the market. "Um…" Her cheeks warmed and she stared at her feet.

"What if I give you what Oded gave to his first wife each week?"

She nodded.

He went to the shelves and selected a small cloth drawstring pouch. After dropping a handful of coins into it, he returned to her and held it out.

"And what am I responsible to purchase with this?"

He shook his head. "Nothing. Diana and Sopha buy whatever the house needs. This is for you. Every week."

"For…?"

"Whatever you want. Perfume—though obviously there is plenty of that here. Wool, silk, yarn. Jewelry. You can find almost anything there." He dropped the pouch into her palm. "Oded is nothing if not generous." He returned to the table and picked up a reed pen, making marks on a long piece of parchment.

"What are you writing?"

"The amount I gave you."

"Do I need to tell you what I bought?"

His brows furrowed. "No, of course not. Why would you?" He pointed to the parchment with the end of his reed pen. "I just keep track of Oded's money. How much comes in, how much goes out. I pay what he owes, sometimes I collect what he is due. He always knows exactly how much he has at any given moment."

"Oh." In Bethany, Simeon was responsible to tell others how much he spent and what he received for his coins. Then again, that money belonged to the whole village, not one man.

"Thank you." Yana headed for the door.

"Stay near Basya," he called as she exited. "She'll make sure you don't pay too much."

Basya rushed back down the stairs and grabbed her hand. "Let's go."

The agora was only a few streets away, so moments later they strolled under the arch that marked the entrance, with soaring towers on either side. The other three sides of the market were covered porticos, tall columns holding up the roof, shops crammed together. Men and women bustled in every direction like ants, crossing from one stall to another.

The scents of ground spices, freshly spun woolen thread, and roasted meat filled the air. The chaos was only slightly less than that of the market in the south of the city, but it was certainly cleaner and brighter.

"Do you have any yarn? Bring any with you?"

Yana shook her head. "Was I supposed to?"

"The rabbis say servants can do the grinding and baking, washing, even preparing the ba'al's bed, but even a woman with one hundred servants must weave so she doesn't become idle." She laughed. "You can spin the wool as well or buy the yarn and weave only."

"I've always hated the spinning."

"Might as well take advantage then and buy it." She led Yana to the section of the upper market where the wool merchants displayed their wares. "There are more colors and more varieties on the market street near the temple, but I would never go there." She grimaced. "If there is something in particular you want from there, you can ask the servants and they can bring it for you."

Yana's eyes skimmed the rows of natural wool, dyed wool, and dyed bundles of silk and linen yarn in addition to wool. Other than madder red, weld yellow, and blue from woad, she'd only seen—and worn—wool just as it came from the sheep. "Let's try some of this." She pointed to some woolen yarn in a bright red. "Some of that, please."

The vendor picked up a large skein. "One? Or more?"

"I'll start with one."

He raised an eyebrow. "The color might not match if you buy more later."

She nodded. "One."

The yarn in his fist, he quoted a price. Yana reached for her pouch, but Basya put her hand over Yana's, offering half of what he asked.

He laughed, dropping his price a fraction. Basya countered. Back and forth the numbers went until they agreed. Yana handed over the coins and he relinquished the yarn, grumbling and complaining under his breath as he counted.

They wandered farther down the row of stalls. Yana leaned near to Basya. "I think we angered him," she whispered.

Basya grinned. "Look back at him."

The vendor was pouring the coins from one palm to another, grinning from ear to ear.

"It's all part of shopping at a market. The bargaining, the badgering, even the arguing. They love it. They'll make you feel like you are stealing food from their baby's mouth when they know they're asking for far more than they could ever get." She pointed ahead. "Let's try to match this color for me. This place is good for wool, but for silk and linen I go to someone else." She stopped at another stall, holding skeins next to her own, hunting for a perfect match.

"What do you plan to do with it tomorrow?" asked Yana.

"Do with what?"

She pointed to the yarn in Basya's fist. "You said you needed to match yarn for tomorrow."

"Oh, yes. Every second day of the week, Naomi and I and my boys go to her abba's house."

"Her abba? He lives near here?"

Basya frowned. "You don't know who her abba is?"

"No. Oded never said."

"Her abba, Benaiah ben Shammai, is one of the priests of the Sanhedrin. He is second only to Gamaliel, the chief priest." Basya spoke as if Yana were remiss in not knowing this. "He adores the children, so we take them to him one day each week. At his age he's surprisingly healthy."

Yana, not yet having given the priest any great-grandchildren, obviously was not invited.

CHAPTER EIGHT

Two are better than one, because they have a good
return for their labor:
If either of them falls down, one can help the other up.
But pity anyone who falls and has no one to help them up.
~ Ecclesiastes 4:9–10 ~

Month of Kislev
Late Fall, AD 30
Jerusalem

Two weeks. Oded had been gone for two Sabbaths.
Seventeen days.

Yana pulled her cloak a little tighter against the chilled morning air of the rainy season as she watched from the upper hallway. Another messenger stood in the atrium waiting for Alexander to read the parchment.

She held her breath. Would he have any news for her?

Alexander ducked into his room, returning with a separate parchment rolled and tied.

The courier departed. He was at least the fifth man Oded had dispatched from…wherever he was, yet not one sentence, one word, one thought had been meant for her.

Why did he even want a wife if he was never home?

Alexander looked up, wincing.

She retreated into her chamber. The tile floors hoarded the cold, and without the body heat of others to help warm the room, as it had been in Bethany, Yana had added another blanket to her bed at night.

Naomi continued to disapprove of nearly everything Yana did, mocking her accent, pointing out her lack of taste, reminding her of her humble village origins.

A knock sounded on her door.

Why can't you leave me alone?

Yana trudged to the door. What had she done wrong now?

Basya waited in the hall, her back to Yana, facing the temple. "Isn't it beautiful? I love how the morning sun almost makes it look like the whole building is on fire." She sighed contentedly. "Ready for the market?"

Yana really didn't need anything, but she did enjoy Basya's company.

And she had nothing else to do.

As they strolled down the narrow alleyways, Yana's thoughts centered on Oded. What could she do differently? How could she make their marriage better? Or at least tolerable?

"Yana!"

Yana flinched at Basya's sharp voice. "What?"

"Are you listening to me at all?"

Yana grimaced. "I'm so sorry. I wasn't. What were you saying?" They had reached the marketplace, but Yana had no recollection of a single step.

"What has you so preoccupied?"

"Oded."

Basya frowned. "What about him?"

"I wish I knew what he wanted. He seems to have been angry with me since the day we married, and I have no idea what I've done wrong."

"I'm sure he's not angry." Basya slipped her arm through Yana's. "It's difficult to get used to them being gone so much of the time. It was hard for me at first too. But I'm sure it will get better soon."

If it was hard for Basya when Naomi approved of her as a match for Elon, would Yana ever be accepted?

Yet in everything Basya had told Yana so far, she'd been right. She'd have to trust she was right this time too.

The afternoon shadows lengthened, leaving distorted gray shapes on the floor of the atrium.

Oded returned without warning. Yana's only indication that he was back was the clatter mixed with barked orders as bags and chests were dragged and piled inside.

And the smell of camels, waiting in the narrow road to be relieved of their burdens.

Yana waited, hoping he would seek her out, tell her about his trip. Where did he go? What had he done each day for weeks? What spices did he purchase? Was he happy with the price?

The conversation never happened. Oded had his evening meal sent to his workroom and remained behind a closed door until long past sunset.

Yana finally dropped into bed after the Roman trumpets marked the end of the second watch.

She'd waited patiently for three weeks for his return.

She needn't have bothered. Everything remained the same whether he was home or not.

A sharp rap at her door awakened her. Was it morning? Was someone hurt? She raced to the door and opened it.

Oded.

"Come," he said.

How could she forget the only thing that changed with his presence?

He turned and headed to his chamber.

She dutifully followed.

When he was done, Yana slunk back to her bed. Why did she feel like one of the women she'd seen near the southern gate, lips too red, cheeks too pink, perfume too strong? Unveiled. Unashamed. Unwanted.

She fell into bed and cried herself to sleep.

Each night for a week, the same scene repeated itself.

By the seventh night, she no longer cried.

Even with his inattention, Yana grew to like the fact that Oded was at least home with her. A marriage couldn't be nurtured with only one person present.

The morning after Sabbath, Yana found Oded in the atrium, adding bags and boxes to a pile on the atrium tiles.

Alexander grabbed the two largest sacks and carried them outside.

What was he doing?

She reached for Oded, but before she could speak he disappeared again into his workroom.

Alexander returned, filling his arms with items from the growing stack.

Yana neared him as he picked up one more bag. "What are—what…?"

The servant hesitated. "He's leaving."

"Leaving?" All the breath rushed from her lungs.

Alexander's face reflected her pain. "I'm sorry," he whispered before ducking back outside.

Oded dropped another box alongside the others.

"You have to leave again?" Yana tried to keep from whining. But how could he go again so soon? They'd had not one conversation.

"My business requires it." He sounded annoyed that he had to explain even that much.

Dare she ask for more? "I'm sorry I don't understand, but can you explain to me why your business requires so much time away from home?" she asked as sweetly, as deferentially as she could.

He drew in a deep breath and halted his packing. "Do you have any idea how I became the most successful spice dealer in all of Jerusalem? In all of Judea?"

"No, I don't. But I'd love to know."

He began to pace, waving his hands as if he were addressing an entire group of people. "Most spices are not grown here in Judea. Our climate and soil are not friendly to most crops. You remember how hard you had to work to coax a sufficient barley crop each year."

She tried to ignore the condescension in his voice. "Yes, I do."

"Imagine fragile, delicate plants being subjected to such conditions. So we get most of our spices from far away—Egypt, Arabia, some even farther. I purchase them from the Nabateans, who refuse to reveal their specific sources." He chuckled softly. "They tell wild stories about obtaining them—giant flying creatures, winged snakes, enormous beasts, jagged mountains. I personally think they are just that—legends created to justify the outrageous prices they command. But be that as it may, they take all the risk and suffer the inconveniences of weeks on the backs of camels, spending days in the brutal desert sun and nights in khans hidden away in the canyons and crevasses to avoid bandits."

"Khans?"

He seemed irritated to have to stop and explain. "Caravansaries. Huge places, with plenty of space and water for the camels, beds and food for the drivers. Now, the problem is, once they reach here, there are many merchants vying for the same load. We outbid each other, drive up the price. So instead of waiting for them to come here, I go to them—in Petra, in Avdat, sometimes elsewhere. In return for promising not to sell to my fellow traders, I get an enormous discount. I can charge less than everyone else and still make much more than they do."

She nodded. "Ah. I see now. Thank you for sharing that information with me."

"In addition to the spices for the incense, I also make perfume. The most sought-after scent is derived from a balsam tree. The Romans adore it and try relentlessly to steal the formula as well as the trees, so most of us who grow the balsam have nurtured groves in Ein Gedi, where they cannot find them. I spend a great deal of time at the oasis there. I have the largest grove by far and many workers there, but I must keep a careful eye on my crop. I retrieve the extract often so my factories here can produce the scent, and I sell it to the Romans for an exorbitant amount." He allowed a light smile. "So you understand why I must be gone so often?"

"I do."

"I'll return in about ten days then." He turned and left without a farewell.

Yana had turned to head for the women's room when Alexander's deep voice stopped her.

"I'm so sorry. I remember how hard it was when I first came to Judea. I left my family, my friends, everything I knew. It must be even worse when the only person you do know is never around." He smiled. "If I can help you at all, please let me know."

"Thank you." She tilted her head. "You don't always travel with him?"

"Occasionally. But I take care of all his finances, and there is much that happens even when he is not here. His brother usually accompanies him, and about once a year they take Basya and the boys with them to Petra."

She would be alone then, here in this enormous city.

Her fear must have registered on her face, for Alexander continued quickly. "That happens rarely. And I'm sure you would go along then as well."

She forced a smile. "Thank you for the information, Alexander."

He grinned. "Everyone calls me Xander."

"Xander. Thank you again."

She allowed him to hold her gaze a little longer than she should have, but she found it hard to resist the warmth in his voice.

CHAPTER NINE

The LORD is close to the brokenhearted
and saves those who are crushed in spirit.
~ Psalm 34:18 ~

Month of Nissan, Passover
Spring, AD 31
Jerusalem, Judea

Yana squeezed her eyes tight to stop the tears that threatened to flood her face. She had truly thought that by Pesach she would be carrying Oded's child.

Each month, for the last six months, he'd made his displeasure achingly clear. Disappointment not only in the fact that she was not pregnant—disappointment in *her*.

She reached for the headscarf that matched her bright yellow tunic and settled it on her head. In the open hallway outside her chamber, she gazed out over the city. Jerusalem teemed with Roman soldiers brought from Caesarea by the governor, Pilate, to handle the Pesach crowds. Soldiers in full armor, spears in hand, lined the bridge from the upper city to the temple. Tears burned the back of her throat as even more men, crimson capes softly waving, stood on the walls of the Temple of Adonai, glaring down at the crowds.

The streets were crammed with people bumping shoulders, filling the streets from edge to edge, creeping slowly toward the temple. The western double gates swung open and the first group—made up naturally of the wealthy merchants from the upper city—paraded under its arches.

Even from here, the iron scent of blood from the lambs that had already been slain and claimed by the heads of families lingered in the air.

Jews believed that Messiah would come to Jerusalem during Pesach, and each year the Holy City swelled to more than five times its size. The city was now simply not big enough to hold them all, so for the days of the feast the priests temporarily extended the official borders of the city to include smaller villages like Bethany and Bethpage.

In the last weeks, the priests had set up ovens all over the city so that those who had journeyed from far away could roast the lamb in the city and eat it as required by the law.

Yana searched for Oded along the bridge. He should have returned long ago. He and Elon had gone to the temple to purchase a lamb and have it slain. After the priests slit its throat and drained the animal of every drop of its precious lifeblood, the brothers would claim the lifeless body and dress it before bringing it home. The skin was left with the priests.

Yana had always waited in Bethany until Simeon and Ezi returned with the sacrificed lamb. The Pesach meal had to be eaten in family groups of at least ten, so Simeon invited not only Yana's family but one other as well, usually the newest residents, to share the meal. While they waited for the men to go in groups of one or two, leading their unblemished lamb to the temple, the women prepared the rest of the meal.

Finally, she glimpsed Oded's favorite blue robe. Elon walked behind him. The lamb's front legs and back legs had been tied together, and each brother had one pair of the animal's feet in his fist as they trudged home with the Passover meal.

Yana hurried down the stone steps to greet him as he entered the atrium. Naomi already waited there. Apparently Sopha had been watching as well, as had her husband, Kronos, because within moments they joined her, ready to receive the lamb and begin the roasting, a process that would take a great deal of the afternoon into the evening.

One of the double doors to Oded's house was kicked open and the pair burst through. Diana and Kronos took the lamb from them then headed toward the back of the house.

"What took so long? It's never taken this long before," asked Naomi.

"There was a deranged man in the temple courts." Elon chuckled. "He upset the tables in the Court of the Gentiles, and the priests stopped their work to get rid of him."

"What do you mean he upset everything? Who is this person?" Naomi stepped closer.

"I heard people calling him Yeshua. I know nothing more of him. He came into the Women's Court, along with eight or ten other men," said Oded. "At first he seemed perfectly normal. I only noticed him because there were so many, and usually there are no more than two at a time to ease the crowding in the courts. He marched to the tables of the money changers and I thought he was going to purchase his lamb. I think they came from Galilee, because most of them had accents." He glanced at Yana as if she were somehow responsible for the actions of all Galileans.

"He changed his money then moved toward the sellers," Oded continued with the story. "I have no idea what happened next. He picked up some of the rope leads lying on the ground and braided them together."

"Then he let all the animals out!" Elon laughed. "The priests changing money were furious! They got up and started screaming at him to stop, but he cracked his little whip and drove all the animals from the courts. Priests were running after them, chasing them down the street!"

"That was bad enough," continued Oded, "but then he toppled all the tables of the money changers and the vendors. Coins scattered everywhere. Levites scurried after them, men and boys dove to retrieve them first, and priests came from everywhere trying to get control."

"Why was he turning over the tables?"

Oded shrugged. "He yelled something about turning his abba's house into a market. I have no idea what that means. The high priest stormed up to him and asked him by what authority he claimed to do all this, and the man said—"

"'Destroy this temple,'" Elon interrupted, "'and I will raise it again in three days.' That's what he said. Have you ever heard anything so preposterous in your life? It's taken forty-six years to build and it's still not done!" Elon roared.

"What did the priests do then?"

"Nothing! The man turned and just walked away."

"He'll disappear, like all the others." Oded slapped his hands together and retreated into his workspace. Elon followed, closing the door behind him. Naomi headed for the stairs.

Yana was left standing alone in the atrium. So far she had spent all of Pesach alone, and it looked like she would spend the rest of it by herself as well, at least until it was time to eat.

Such a far cry from Passovers in Bethany when everyone stayed outdoors, the women preparing the meals together, while the men, only strides away, roasted the lambs. There was joy and singing and laughing as they praised Adonai for delivering them from Egypt and the cruelty of the pharaoh centuries ago. Children chased each other from courtyard to courtyard. Smoke rose from every firepit, and the air filled with the aroma of fire and flesh.

Right now, she would give anything to be back in Bethany.

The silence of evening was broken by the squeals of children, a sound rarely heard in Oded's house. Yana stepped out of her room in time to see Basya's boys run to a stoic old man in the long robe of a priest.

"*Sabba!*"

So this was Naomi's abba, Benaiah ben Shammai.

Their great-grandfather bent and allowed them to kiss his cheeks before returning to the door and allowing his feet to be washed.

The boys turned to two much younger priests who had entered behind the man. Standing tall, the boys bowed their heads. "Shalom, Rabbi Isaac, Rabbi Saul."

The older one—Saul—stepped forward. "Shalom, Abihu, Amariah. Are you ready for Pesach?"

"Yes, Rabbi."

"And did you search the entire house for leaven?"

The boys bobbed their heads like doves pecking at grain.

"The whole house? By candlelight?"

"Yes, Rabbi!"

"Excellent. You have learned well." He smiled broadly and placed a hand on each of their heads.

Oded exited his workroom. "Sabba Benaiah! Shalom."

"Oded." The priest nodded. "Where is my daughter?"

"Probably still getting dressed. She'll be down—" Oded grinned and gestured toward the stairs. "Here she is. Imma, your abba has arrived."

Naomi hurried to the man, who smiled only slightly and spread his arms to just barely embrace her. "My beloved daughter."

No wonder Naomi was always so sour.

Basya drew up beside Yana and touched her arm. "Ready?"

Not really, but there was no other choice.

"Don't worry. They pretty much ignore us, anyway."

Yana nodded and walked with Basya to the stairs. They stepped onto the atrium and followed Oded and the priests into the dining area.

Benaiah took his place at one end of the table. Naomi sat to his right, followed by Oded and Elon. They continued around the table from oldest to youngest. Yana sat beside Abihu.

Candles on the table tossed flickering light on a platter of unleavened bread, roasted vegetables, and a bowl of vinegar. Benaiah picked up the pitcher of wine and struggled to lift it only a hand's breadth above the table, closing his eyes. "Blessed are You, O Lord our God, who has created the fruit of the vine. Blessed are You, O Lord our God, who has kept us alive, sustained us, and enabled us to enjoy this season."

Diana took the pitcher from him and poured a small amount into each person's cup.

Yana sat silently as the traditions were followed. The wine and the blessings, the vegetables dipped in vinegar, the four questions, the breaking of the bread—how was it that everything was exactly as it was in Bethany, and yet nothing was the same?

It isn't the same because there is no joy here.

Abihu and Amariah were careful to say and do everything exactly as required. The women were silent. The men recited words that seemed to have no meaning.

Where was the triumph of the exodus from Egypt, the rescue from slavery? Where was the celebration of family?

Sopha appeared with the roasted lamb.

Benaiah again closed his eyes for the blessing. "Blessed are You, O Lord our God, King of the universe, who brings forth bread from the earth. Blessed are You, O Lord our God, King of the universe, who has sanctified us with Your commandments, and commanded us to eat unleavened bread."

Their ritual nearly done, the boys relaxed. Conversation began to flow.

"Were you at the temple earlier, when that madman chased away the animals?" asked Elon.

"I was." Benaiah huffed. "Disgraceful. That man is going to bring enormous trouble on himself if he's not careful."

"Who is he?" Naomi reached for another piece of lamb.

"He's a rabbi from Nazareth, as I understand." Benaiah sipped his wine. "I don't know why he thinks he has authority to tell the sons of Aaron how temple business should be conducted. Galileans! They don't even keep the law properly themselves."

Once again, Yana could feel Oded's stare, but she concentrated on her meal.

"The people seem to love him though," said Oded.

Benaiah laughed. "Of course they do! He promises them a new kingdom, and a new temple built in three days!"

"Can he perform such miraculous deeds?" Naomi laughed.

"There are those," said Isaac, "who say he changed water to wine in Cana recently." The young rabbi cringed when Benaiah glared at him.

Benaiah smacked the table with his open hand. "No one can do that. It is merely a lie to get the people behind him."

"If he gets too many behind him, Rome will intervene," added Saul.

"I know. We cannot allow that." Benaiah pursed his lips.

"Well, what will you do?" asked Oded.

"I don't know yet. But he must be stopped." Benaiah slowly shook his head, eyes flashing. "He simply must be stopped. Whatever it takes."

CHAPTER TEN

Wait for the LORD;
be strong and take heart and wait for the LORD.
~ Psalm 27:14 ~

Month of Av
Midsummer, AD 31
Jerusalem, Judea

Late into the night, unable to sleep, Yana paced in the women's room, chewing her nails, afraid to breathe. She should have seen her red flow over two weeks ago. Had Adonai finally answered her prayers?

When should she tell Oded? Many pregnancies ended before the third month, so should she wait until she thought it was safe? Perhaps it would be better to tell him as soon as he arrived home tomorrow, so he would at least know it was possible for her to conceive.

She went back and forth between telling and not telling until she was exhausted. She climbed the stairs to her chamber and fell into bed. She could decide tomorrow, or even the day after.

In the dark of night, gut-wrenching cramps awakened her. With her arms wrapped around her belly as if she could protect the child within, she crawled out of bed and stumbled to the little room downstairs where the family went to relieve themselves.

For once she thought having such a room indoors was a great idea.

Hands shaking, she lit a candle and then pulled off her simple sleeping tunic.

Bright crimson saturated her undergarment.

No, no, no, no…

The ache of disappointment and grief strangled her, robbing her of breath, her physical pain dwindling in comparison.

Why, Adonai?

She lay on the tile floor, hugging herself, begging Him to answer, but He wasn't talking.

At least not to her.

Yana slept late the next morning. She'd been up the rest of the night, gnawing cramps—and numbing despair—robbing her of sleep. Finally, just before the sun rose, the pain had subsided and she'd mercifully drifted off.

After a fitful couple of hours of rest, she rose and put on a clean tunic. She moved to the window and opened the wooden shutter. The midmorning sun shone down on creation just as it had yesterday. Birds twittered, people chatted as they strolled back and forth across the bridge, a gentle warm breeze swirled dust along the street.

Her chest tightened. How did life go on just as before? It was nothing like before. She was empty, bereft, barren.

Useless.

Month after month, for nearly a year, she had failed to become pregnant. And when she finally did conceive, she proved unable to keep the baby alive. The one thing women were created to do without even thinking.

Why was she incapable of doing what came so naturally to every other woman?

The front door opened.

Yana peeked out of her door in time to see Oded storm in. She hadn't expected him until later. This time of day he should be at his perfume shops, or even at Ein Gedi. He strode to the middle of the atrium and looked up, beckoning.

A chill began in her belly and spread to her arms and legs. She willed herself to descend the stairs to meet him.

Hands behind his back, he strolled toward her. "You lost the baby?"

Shock slammed into her. She hadn't even told him yet that she was pregnant. How did he find out so fast she'd lost it?

She bowed her head. "Yes, Ba'ali. Last night."

"What did you do to cause this?"

She stepped back as if she'd been struck. "What did *I* do?"

He crossed his arms over his chest. "Yes. You must have done something."

She blew out a sharp breath. "I did nothing. It's quite common to lose a pregnancy this early. Especially the first one."

He snarled. "Is it *common* for the first one to take so long to begin with?"

His words sliced through her. Could he hurt her any more deeply?

"I'm sorry." What else could she do but apologize?

Even though it was not her fault.

He scoffed, then turned and strode into his workroom.

Yana stood there, feeling naked and exposed. She was ashamed and she wasn't even sure why.

Diana came beside her. "Come with me." She grabbed Yana's hand and led her toward the dining area. In the right-hand corner was a small doorway she'd never noticed before. Not that she'd actually spent much time in the room. Diana led her outside into a wide courtyard with a dirt floor. The other three sides of the space were bounded by low stone walls. A long table, covered with baskets of fruit, vegetables, and the day's bread, sat against the wall of the dining area behind them. Shelves full of platters, bowls, plates, and cups lined the right side, while two ovens stood next to several stone water jars on the left.

Diana walked to the table and retrieved a plate of sliced fruit. "I was going to bring this to you, but then the ba'al returned." She glanced at Yana's belly, her eyes misting. "I'm so sorry."

"Thank you." Yana picked out a slice of pale orange melon and bit into it. The sweet juice slid down her throat.

"More?" Diana held out the platter.

"Yes, pl—"

Yana's chest constricted as footsteps sounded in the dining area. Had Oded come looking for her?

"Diana, did you—" Xander halted just inside the doorway. He caught Yana's gaze, glanced around, and took a step back. "I'm sorry. Please forgive me."

Yana relaxed. A bit. "For what?"

"I didn't mean to intrude on you. I didn't know you were in here."

"You didn't intrude. This is your space. You should feel free to come as you please."

"Still—"

Yana pointed a thumb at the young servant. "Diana brought me back."

He stepped closer and his face darkened. "She told me what happened."

"That I lost our baby or that Oded blamed me for it?"

His mouth fell open.

She winced. She shouldn't have snapped at him. "I'm sorry. I didn't mean to speak ill of my husband. I haven't slept much."

Shaking his head, Xander accepted a plate of fruit from Diana. "He shouldn't treat you that way." He almost seemed to be mumbling to himself.

He was right. Oded shouldn't treat her this way. But he did, and there wasn't anything she could do to change that.

Xander leaned back against the table facing her, crossing one foot over the other. "But at least you've got time. He can't do to you what he did to his first wife. Not for ten years anyway." He downed another slice of melon.

Her breath caught. "Did to his first wife? I thought she died." Surely Xander didn't mean Oded had killed her.

He chuckled dryly. "Died? No. Is that what he told you?"

"Xander..." Diana grabbed his arm.

Yana tried to remember if Oded had ever said anything about her. "Come to think of it, I don't think he ever said anything. I just assumed she had died."

Xander shook his head and remained silent.

She clenched her fist. He couldn't say something like that and not explain himself. "Well, what happened?"

"Maybe I shouldn't say anything more."

"Tell me!"

He allowed a hint of a smile at her impatience. "The ba'al divorced her when she did not produce an heir."

Her stomach sank to her bare feet. She'd heard that was possible, but she'd never known anyone who'd done it, or even heard of anyone who had. That explained so many comments by Basya. And why Naomi hushed her every time they got too close to the subject.

"No children? Or no sons?"

"No children. After ten years."

Was this what was in store for Yana? A divorce? Because she couldn't give him a child? And only after nine more years filled with his neglect and anger?

"Why is it so important he have a son? I understand every man wants a child, but it seems far more important to him than most."

Xander set aside his plate. "Oded has built a very successful business. It truly is remarkable. But he needs a son to pass it on to."

"Every man wants an heir—"

He raised one hand, palm out. "No, you don't understand. He is the sole supplier of several of the ingredients that make up the holy incense in your temple. The Avtinas—the family that makes the incense and keeps the secret recipe—are afraid that if Oded doesn't control the balsam groves in Ein Gedi, Rome will seize them again."

"Again?"

"Marcus Antoninus confiscated the groves from King Herod and gave them to Cleopatra as a gift about one hundred years ago. The Romans love the perfume it makes— they say it drives men wild." He smiled and shrugged. "The Hasmoneans recaptured Ein Gedi, and now Oded stations armed guards to keep away enemies and visitors alike. The groves are somewhere near the oasis, hidden from sight behind palm groves. He comes and goes at night. At any rate, Oded must have an heir to inherit his trade and keep his secrets."

"Couldn't he make his nephews his heirs?"

"He could, but you know how prideful he is."

She nodded.

So this was why he was always so cold to her. It wasn't that they needed to learn to love one another. He'd never intended to love her, so why bother spending any time with her at all? Other than when trying to get her pregnant?

At least now she knew. Now she could quit trying to please him. She would never be able to.

Yana dropped her tunic and undergarments onto the floor behind her and placed her feet on the top stone step of the mikveh. She continued, counting twelve steps, the water level climbing up her body until she was fully under the water. She tried to drown out the words her mind shouted at her. *"There is no baby. There is no baby. And it's your fault. You are a failure."*

Unable to be touched, trapped not only in her house but in her chamber or the women's room, the twelve days of impurity each month kept her isolated, a painful reminder of her inability to conceive. This time, it was longer than usual, as the miscarriage took over a week to complete. Add another seven days and she'd been alone for over two weeks.

She turned and ascended the stairs, dried, and dressed in clean clothes. Her days of uncleanness were complete.

Perhaps a visit to her cousins would cheer her, take her mind off losing the baby. She hadn't seen them since the wedding, and just the thought of Bethany always lifted her spirits. But Basya and Naomi were at Benaiah's house, and a woman traveling alone was not only vulnerable, but she also gave the wrong impression. Who would accompany her?

What about Diana? Would she be allowed to set aside her duties for a day?

Surprised but delighted when Diana obtained permission from Sopha, Yana soon led her east toward the market street that ran along the western wall of the temple and to the southern gate. "I know Basya says she never comes to the lower market, but I like it here. The people are more like me, not like..."

"My brother comes here often. He says the prices are lower and the quality is just as good if not better. And he says they have items here he can't find at the upper market."

"Your brother?"

Diana's brow furrowed. "Xander."

"Xander is your brother?" She'd had no idea.

"You didn't know?"

"No. The two of you always appeared closer than simply servants in the same household, but I thought maybe—"

"Eeew! No!"

The girl's horrified face made Yana laugh. "Sorry."

After she turned south, the street came alive. Noise and crowds buffeted them like waves. Yana had forgotten the second and sixth days of the week were busier here. When the craftsmen joined the food merchants, the number of active shops doubled, and the number of those seeking bargains tripled. She reached for Diana. "Grab my hand so we don't get separated."

People rushed to and fro, buying not only the day's food but pottery, cloth, sandals, whatever was necessary and available.

She tried to remember where she had seen the dyed wool when she entered Jerusalem that first day. Images of women weaving as they waited for customers came to mind. All the women were south of the temple, closer to the gate.

They strolled by the stalls. Most were run by merchants, or more likely their servants. The same colors, with varying intensities, were at each shop. Reds, indigos, yellows.

"I don't see anything different than what I saw at the upper market. Let's go."

On their way out of the gate, they passed a shop that was smaller than the others but immaculate. Yana slowed as she passed. An older woman, hunched and wrinkled, sat on the ground before a cloth covered with skeins of yarn. The same brilliant yellows, bright crimsons, and earthy browns were there, but also some unique colors.

Yana knelt before the cloth, fingering the yarn.

The woman's face brightened with a wide smile. Apparently she didn't get a lot of business. "Shalom. May Adonai bless you."

"Shalom." Yana returned the smile.

The woman had skin the color of walnuts and hair whiter than the undyed wool she offered. Her hands were curled up in pain. How did she complete her work with so little movement in her fingers?

"You have so many interesting colors. I don't see them anywhere else."

"Thank you, ba'alah."

Yana shook her head. "Please don't call me that."

The woman cackled. "Everyone from the upper city expects to be addressed in this way. That is, if they ever venture down here. Most send their servants, but even they expect a good deal of deference."

Diana shook her head. "She hates it."

"Just call me Yana."

"Then you may call me Ketziah."

"How did you achieve this color?" Yana pointed to a skein the color of fire.

"That started out as ordinary yellow. I had some red dye from carmine but not enough to dye even a tunic, so I added it to the weld. Isn't it beautiful?"

"Carmine?"

"It's made from bugs."

Yana frowned, and the woman laughed again.

"I'll take all you have."

Her eyes lit up with amazement. "You will?"

"I hate spinning yarn, but I am required to weave. I think this bright color will make the task far more pleasant."

"Then I pray for your peace as you make something beautiful. You must come share the finished product with me."

"I'd be delighted to do that."

Diana accepted the skeins from Ketziah and dropped them into a bag while Yana reached into her sash to pull out a tiny pouch. She opened it and stuck a finger inside to get an idea of how much she carried. More than enough.

"I have four more." The woman gestured with one twisted finger behind her. "Do you really want it all, or just what I have here?"

Yana could feel people watching. Women dressed as she was did not lurk about the lower city. "It's beautiful. I'll take it all, before someone else steals it from me."

Another laugh, whether from Yana's attempt at humor or at her good fortune Yana couldn't tell. The woman stuffed the other skeins in the bag and quoted the price.

Yana pulled the strings on her little pouch and handed it to the woman. "May I ask you something?"

"Of course." The woman laid the pouch in her lap.

"How do you accomplish all this"—she waved her hand over the yarns—"with your hands as they are? I know dying yarn takes a good deal of strength."

"Very observant of you." She grinned. "I live with my daughter and her son. My daughter and I are both widowed. She stays home and does the hard work while I sit up here charming people into buying more yarn than they need." She grinned, showing a missing tooth.

"You do a very good job of it." Yana rose. "I'll be back." She spoke a little louder than necessary.

"I hope so."

Diana grabbed her arm. "You gave her all your money?"

"It's worth it."

They'd not taken very many steps when the old woman squealed. Yana looked over her shoulder to see people crowding around the tiny shop.

A smile crossed her face. It had been a long while since she'd helped someone. It felt good.

CHAPTER ELEVEN

Children are a heritage from the LORD,
offspring a reward from him.
~ Psalm 127:3 ~

Month of Elul
Late Summer, AD 31
Jerusalem, Judea

Yana tied the sash around her waist.

She was afraid to breathe. Afraid to hope.

After almost a year, had Adonai finally answered her prayers?

Oded had nearly reached the end of his patience with her. No matter how she tried to impress upon him that Adonai alone granted the gift of a child, Oded continued to blame her, acting as if she were refusing to get pregnant out of spite.

Yet he was the one who had been married for ten years with no success.

Not that she would dare point that out.

If only he knew how much a child would add to her life. Son or daughter, she would have someone to love, someone to care for, someone who would love her back. To fill her days with purpose and joy. To give some meaning to her desolate existence.

She settled a hand on her belly. Was there a child inside her? Would he live long enough to feel the sun on his face?

Adonai, please grant me this child.

"I'm going to the market. Want to join me?"

Yana jumped at the sound of Basya's voice.

"I'm sorry. I didn't hear the door open."

Basya neared her and placed a hand on her arm. "Are you all right?"

She plastered on a bright smile. A smile she didn't feel. "Of course. Let's go."

In the market, Yana slowed as they passed the spice section. Ground and whole spices precariously piled high in cloth bags, all but overflowing, were displayed in neat rows. She'd worked hard to learn the appearance and names of the seasonings so she could understand Oded's life.

He never spoke to her about his business, but she would be prepared if he ever decided to trust her.

Tiny hard balls of black, white, green, and pink: peppercorns. Bright orange threads: saffron. Rolls of fragrant bark: cinnamon. Translucent nuggets of gum resin: frankincense.

"You don't have enough spices at home?" Basya laughed. "Let's get some oil."

Plain olive oil was bought by the servants in the lower market, where basic commodities were sold. But here in the upper market the vendors had scented oils—oils infused with balsam, honey, and myrrh, which the wealthy women of Jerusalem used to soften their skin and bring a shine to their hair.

She might as well enjoy the luxuries Oded's success allowed her if she could enjoy nothing else of her life in the Holy City.

She picked up a small, open amphora and removed the cloth laid loosely over it. She sniffed. Jasmine. Another smelled of cinnamon and a third of vanilla. Oded's favorite, and the most expensive.

Holding the jar of vanilla oil, she gestured to the vendor. "I'll take some of this. And I want your best."

"That is my best." An oily smile adorned his face.

She held his gaze. "I know you keep the finest oil in the back."

He glowered at her but reached behind a curtain to retrieve a larger glass bottle with a stopper, then quoted a price.

"I'll give you half that. No more."

He sputtered and fumed but held out his hand.

"You've learned well." Basya chuckled. "Figs should be out by now. Elon loves fresh figs."

Four of the vendors had early figs. Basya set about comparing the figs and the prices, haggling for the best deal.

Yana had no energy to toss prices back and forth with the vendors today. "Six, please." She pulled out coins as the man dropped the green fruit into her basket.

The vendor kept his hand out.

Basya glanced at the figs and the coins. "A little more," she whispered.

"No. That's all I'll pay. Or take back the figs."

The merchant retrieved one of the figs, snarling, leaving her with five.

Basya pulled her away. "What is the matter with you? You're always so generous with Oded's money."

Yana shrugged.

"What is it?" Concern filled Basya's eyes.

Yana closed her eyes. "I think I am with child," she whispered.

Basya squealed.

Yana quickly scanned the faces of those near them to see if anyone reacted. "You cannot say anything. To *anyone.*" She closed her eyes. "I'm so afraid something will happen and I will lose it again."

"Oh, Yana." Basya enveloped her in a tight hug. She pulled back. "How long has it been? Since your last time of blood?"

"Over two months."

"And Oded doesn't know?"

"He probably does, but he hasn't said anything."

"That sounds like him." Basya smirked, then her eyes widened and the smile disappeared. "I'm so sorry. I didn't mean to offend you. Or him."

"You should know by now how I feel about him." She sighed. "He makes no secret of how he feels about me."

"I think he's just overly worried about having an heir. Maybe a baby will change his mind." She threaded her arm through Yana's.

Or make me of no value at all. "Maybe."

"I know! Let's get some silk cloth so you can make a blanket."

Yana frowned. "Silk? For an infant?"

Basya grinned. "Oded would want only the best."

"I'd rather make the cloth myself."

"Why?" Basya scoffed.

She shrugged. "I have to weave something. Might as well be something for the baby." She smiled, allowing herself to imagine what she'd buried in the depths of her mind for so long. "The first time I hold him, I want to wrap him in something I made with my own hands."

"I still think you should get some cloth, just in case he objects."

"Oded will understand."

Basya raised a brow. "If you say so."

Even Oded couldn't object to a mother weaving a blanket for her son.

Could he?

Month of Tishri
Early Fall, AD 31
Bethany, Judea

It had been four months. Surely she wouldn't lose the baby now.

Would it be safe to visit Bethany? The air had cooled, so the journey would be pleasant. Miriam and Marta didn't even know she was with child.

Diana could join her. If they arrived around midday, the girls would be home from their visit to the bet, preparing the evening meal.

Joy-laden memories flooded her. She quickened her steps as they entered the village and continued down the road.

Diana glanced at her. "Your smile is so bright. You loved it here very much, I think."

"I did. I wanted to stay here forever."

The bet lay to their right. As soon as she saw Imma, she would come back to visit the widows.

She nearly broke into a run when the courtyard came into sight, but when she reached it, she found it empty.

"Where is everyone?" Diana frowned. "Is everyone in the fields?"

"No, that can't be it." Except for olives, the harvest was over, and Yana had noticed no one on the mount.

She crossed to her house and stepped inside. It, too, was empty. No pots, jars, or shoes. She peeked into the broadroom. No food, no clothes.

She stepped back into the bright sunlight of the open area. Where were they?

"Yana!" Miriam's eternally cheerful voice drifted in from the road. She burst into a run and headed straight for Yana.

Yana turned to meet her. "Miriam! Where is everyone?"

She gestured loosely toward the fields south of the village. "The donkey got loose, so everyone was trying to track it down. They found him, but he'd fallen in a hole and we were getting him out." She turned to Diana. "Shalom. Diana, right?"

Diana dipped her head. "Shalom."

Simeon approached, leading a donkey covered with mud.

"He's unharmed?" Miriam drew her free hand down the animal's neck.

"A little skittish, but no broken bones. No wounds."

"Thank Adonai! I don't know what we'd do without you." Miriam placed a soft kiss on his nose.

Yana looked beyond Simeon to the road. "Uncle, are my imma and Lemuel coming?"

Simeon's brows formed a V between his eyes. "You didn't receive word? She said she would send you a message."

"What message? Saying what?"

He winced, his gaze settling over her head. "That they were leaving for Galilee."

All the air left her lungs. "Galilee? Why would she go there?"

Simeon rubbed his hand down his face. "Lemuel wanted to return there. I think he was counting on his new connections with your husband to help him sell his wine. I guess when it didn't happen, he decided to go back and work with his brother."

"I—I heard nothing." Her mind raced. Why wouldn't Imma have told her? Or maybe she did but Oded kept the message from her.

Marta came from the house and hugged Yana before grabbing her hand and pulling her inside. "Come, both of you. We'll get you something to eat."

They entered the common room of Simeon's house. She'd always considered Simeon's house extravagant compared to theirs. His floor was tile, not packed dirt. His walls were plastered, not bare stone. He had straw-stuffed mattresses, not reed mats.

Compared to Oded's house, it wasn't that grand. No brightly colored mosaics on the floors. No frescos on the walls. No stone tables. But somehow it felt more like home than where she now lived—had lived for a year and a half.

The table was already piled with warm bread, grapes, figs, and goat cheese. They talked about the bet, the crops, the village, but Yana hesitated to ask the question that had been on her mind since she entered Bethany.

She cleared her throat. "Has anyone heard from Ezi?"

Simeon's smile faded. "When he was in Galilee, he met a teacher, and he's become one of his disciples. He's visited here a couple of times with the teacher and the other followers, but they're usually traveling, sometimes for weeks. We don't see him much."

Fear crawled down her spine. "Not one of those calling people to revolt and rise up against Rome? The... What are they called?"

Simeon raised a brow. "The *zealots*? No, of course not." He shook his head. "This man calls for loving Adonai and those around you, not only your neighbors but your enemies. He's said nothing so far I find that contradicts the law."

It wasn't unusual for a rabbi to have a group of disciples or even for them to go on teaching tours.

It just didn't sound like something Ezi would do.

Then again, she hadn't seen him for over a year.

Month of Adar
Late Winter, AD 31
Jerusalem, Judea

Yana rose from the couch in the women's room as Sopha walked in, a platter of white stone cups in one hand. But before Yana could stand, searing pain knocked her to her knees like a physical punch. Her breath came fast. With her weight on one hand, the other cradled around the belly that threatened to rip in two, she groaned.

Basya jumped up and ran to her. "Yana? What's wrong? Is it the baby?"

Naomi rose, as if nothing had happened. "Sopha, bring some clean cloths and as much cool water as you can carry."

"Yes, ba'alah."

Water and cloths? How were they to help? She didn't need to wash; she needed to stop the pain or she would never survive this.

"Have you been having pains all morning? It doesn't usually begin so strongly." Naomi's voice was sharp, as always.

"They started last night, but they weren't that bad. Just fleeting sharp jabs. Nothing like this."

"You should have said something."

This is the time you choose to chastise me?

"Basya..." Naomi turned her attention to her other daughter-in-law, who was rubbing Yana's back.

"Basya!"

Basya started and looked up to Naomi.

"Help me get her into her own room. The men don't need to hear her cries."

The pain subsided just in time for Yana to allow Basya and Naomi to pull her to her feet and lead her to the bottom of the stairs. Halfway up she stopped, doubling over and leaning on the steps above her. When she could again stand, they hurried her into her room where she collapsed onto her bed.

"Not there!" Naomi barked, and Yana stood, unsteady on her feet. Naomi pointed to Basya. "Go find Sopha and hurry her along and then get a straw mattress." Basya scampered from the room.

Yana had assisted in many births. In Bethany she'd seen the women in pain, heard their cries. Seen their faces. She'd thought she understood what would be happening. But no one had prepared her for the agony that now coursed through her body. Perhaps that was why she'd ignored it throughout the night and all morning.

"Thank you, I'll carry it in." Basya's voice drifted in from the doorway. Apparently one of the male servants had brought the mattress up the stairs for her. The coarse cloth slid across the tiled floor, a scraping sound mixed with Basya's heavy breaths as she dragged the mattress to the center of the room.

Yana lowered herself to the mattress as a gush of water soaked her legs.

She panted as she waited for another contraction. This pain would not be worth it unless she could give her husband a son.

Murky light streaming in her window signaled that the sun had risen once again. The contractions had grown even stronger and more frequent through the night. The neck of her tunic was wet, her face was drenched in sweat, her hair matted to her forehead.

Basya drew a damp cloth over her face. "It won't be long now."

"On your feet. It's time." Naomi slipped an arm under her and helped her sit up while Basya moved to kneel behind Yana.

"Sit on my knees and lean against me," Basya whispered.

Naomi pushed Yana's tunic up to her waist, and Basya grabbed a handful of the fabric and shoved it behind Yana's back to keep it out of the way. The older woman crouched before her. "The head is making its way out. I need you to push!"

Yana grabbed Basya's hands and pushed as hard as she could.

Adonai, please give me a son.

Yana pushed with every contraction, with barely time to catch her breath between them.

Naomi looked up. "One more and we'll have his head."

"It gets much easier after that," Basya added.

Thank Adonai. She didn't think she could endure much more.

"Push!"

Yana groaned as she concentrated all her energy on forcing this little one from her. She felt the baby's head slip from her body.

"Very good, Yana. Rest a moment." Basya drew a cool, damp cloth over her face again.

Her chest heaving, Yana dropped her head back against Basya's chest.

"Oh no." Naomi's voice was barely audible.

Yana sat up as much as she could. "What? What's wrong?"

"The cord is wrapped around his neck."

Panic tightened around her chest like a rope. "What? Will he choke? What do we do?" She couldn't lose this baby. Not now.

Not again.

"Hush!"

Yana flinched at the reprimand.

"Just relax a moment. Let me work." Naomi's voice softened. "Whatever you do, don't push until I've freed the cord from his neck."

"Naomi delivered my babies She knows what she is doing. All will be well," assured Basya.

Yana could feel the older woman's hands move quickly below her.

Adonai, please...

Another wave of pain swept through her, along with an overwhelming urge to push the baby from her body. She gritted her teeth, pushing against the floor with her feet and against Basya with her shoulders.

"Good girl. Don't push."

"Done!" Naomi called triumphantly. "Push now!"

All the force Yana had poured into resisting she now let loose. She felt what must be his shoulders pass through her.

"Almost there. One more, I think."

Yana caught her breath just before the next contraction. She pushed once more.

"He's free!" Naomi nearly laughed as she pulled the baby into her lap. "Oh..."

Now what? "Is he...?"

"He is a *she*." The disappointment dripped from her voice.

Yana resisted apologizing. Adonai reserved the right to give sons, or withhold them. She had no power to do either.

The sharp scents of olive oil and salt swirled around her as Naomi wordlessly rubbed them into the babe's skin. She then wrapped long lengths of linen around her body and handed her to Yana.

Yana stared at the babe in her arms, unable to feel any of the regret that was all over Naomi's face.

She had a baby. A daughter.

How could she be sad about that?

CHAPTER TWELVE

As a father has compassion on his children,
so the LORD has compassion on those who fear him.
~ Psalm 103:13 ~

Yana gazed at her daughter—her perfect, beautiful *daughter*. As she had been promised, every scrap of pain evaporated like morning dew after just one moment with her child.

She peeked beneath the swaddling wrap and counted toes, fingers. Drew her fingers over smooth, silky skin, tiny lips, a nose no bigger than a raisin.

"She's beautiful, Yana." Basya stroked the babe's tiny head and smiled. "Just beautiful."

The infant squirmed and turned her head toward Yana, her mouth open. She moved her head back and forth against her tunic, and suddenly Yana's breasts felt tingly and overfull.

"She's hungry. You need to feed her." Naomi spoke as if telling a servant what she wanted from the market.

"Here, let me help you." Basya pulled the sweaty tunic over Yana's head and tossed it into a basket across the room.

Yana helped the baby find her breast, and she immediately began to suckle. A sharp pain passed quickly, and the baby sucked down a mouthful of milk.

Yana gasped and looked at Basya. Could anything be so amazing?

Basya laughed quietly. "I know. It's an incredible feeling. Such a tiny being, totally dependent on you for everything except her next breath."

"We'll finish cleaning up the room and you while you feed her. Once she is satisfied, you both can rest." Naomi opened the wooden shutters. "And let's get some fresh air in here."

Basya gathered the wet and bloody cloths into the basket with Yana's tunic. With a clean, damp cloth, she once again wiped down Yana's face and neck then each arm, while Naomi cleaned the rest of her aching body. Naomi held out a clean tunic before she left the room with the basket.

Basya helped Yana put it on. "This one has a slit and a tie at the neck to help you feed her easily."

When the infant began to fuss, Yana switched her to the other side, watching in wonder as she gulped down mouthful after mouthful of nourishment.

Naomi returned. "All right, into bed now. You can both get some sleep." Naomi held the infant while Basya helped Yana stand and led her to the raised bed. She sank onto it, more grateful than usual for the wool-stuffed mattress Oded had purchased. She rolled on her side and pulled the babe close to her chest, her arm wrapped around the tiny body of her perfect daughter.

Her daughter.

What would Oded say? Naturally, he'd be disappointed. But they would have more children, and he would be patient.

At least that's what she told herself.

Yana awoke as the door to her room slammed open.

Oded stood in the doorway, face sour. He stared across the room at her for several long moments before he strode toward her. "It's true?" He glared down at the sleeping newborn.

She blinked against the sunlight that now filled the room. "What's true?"

"You delivered a female."

She smiled. "Yes. You have a beautiful daughter." She pulled the blanket away so he could see her face.

"*Not*"—his voice lingered on the word—"a son, then."

"Well, no, but there—"

"I wanted a son. I *need* a son." He stalked to the other side of the room and spun to face her. "I was at my balsam groves when a messenger arrived telling me you were delivering our child. I rushed here on a camel to greet a son. You have wasted my time." Crossing his arms, he spoke as if she had deliberately given him a daughter just to irritate him. "I don't like wasting time." His voice was low and measured, a sure sign he was angry.

"Perhaps next time Adonai will grant us a son." She slipped an arm under the sleeping bundle and held her up to face him. "Would you like to hold her?"

"No." He frowned. "What is that you have her wrapped in? It's hideous."

Yana's stomach roiled. "It's a blanket. I wove it for her."

"It should be silk, or at least linen. She looks like a villager." He turned to go.

Wait. What could she say? What could she offer? "Would you like to name her?" Mothers more often named their children, but perhaps it would please him.

"No." He left without halting or turning around.

Yana dropped her head onto the cushion. Had she really expected a different reaction? She'd tried to convince herself Oded would be just as happy with a daughter, even when her heart told her differently.

How could he be so unfeeling? So unwilling to love a daughter?

Perhaps it was just shock and he would change his mind later. Come back and accept her. Love her.

But Yana knew better. The stories Diana had told her hovered in the back of her mind. Would he send her away as well? How many chances would he give her before he divorced her? The law said she had ten years, but Oded hadn't given the impression he would allow that amount of time to pass before he decided that she, too, was worthless.

She caressed the babe's cheek. Her daughter needed a name—a name that spoke of her preciousness, her supreme importance, her unending value, even though she was not a son but merely a daughter, whose mother was a common woman from a tiny town. Her father was rich, successful, influential. Almost royalty here in Jerusalem.

And if he was royalty then so was the baby.

Sarai? *My princess.* A perfect name for a perfect baby.

Month of Sivan
Late Spring, AD 32
Jerusalem, Judea

Yana stood in the arched doorway of Oded's office and inhaled. The sweet, spicy scents of cinnamon and cloves saturated the air. Light spilled into the room through the four windows that lined the far wall, Roman glass scattering various colors across the floor.

About the same size as the dining area, the room was longer than it was deep. The high ceilings gave an impression of even more space. A deep brown worktable—acacia wood like the dining table—sat at each end of the room. The table at the far end was covered in parchments and wax tables. The one near the doorway contained boxes of various sizes, some jeweled, some wooden, some metal.

"You sent for me, Ba'ali?"

He glanced at her. "Come."

She obeyed.

He drew near to stand before her. "Since you have failed to deliver to me a son, I have been forced to make a difficult decision."

She drew in a sharp breath.

"I plan to hire a nurse to feed the child for you. I understand it is most difficult to conceive while nursing an infant."

Yana's blood turned as cold as the stone on which she stood. "Please, please, no..." She backed away, wishing she could flee his terrible pronouncement.

He shook his head as he paced the length of his office. "I cannot wait another three years to even try to conceive, only to have *you* take another year to become with child and most of yet another for you to carry it."

Her heart raced. Her breathing came fast and shallow, and she fought the feeling that she was suffocating. "But, Ba'ali, I am not the one who chooses whether our child will be a son or daughter! Adonai alone claims that privilege. The scriptures tell us that it is Adonai who opens a woman's womb and who closes it. I have done everything I can do to make it possible to carry a son. I cannot tell you how it grieves me I did not give you a son, and I wish you could embrace our daughter as you would have a son, but even if you can't—"

"Silence!" he roared. He held out a hand, palm toward her, eyes shooting daggers. "You should be happy that I am allowing you to raise this daughter at all." He calmed, then clasped his hands behind his back as he stalked the length of his room. "The Romans have it right. When a father decides a child is unworthy of life he simply places it by the road, allowing it to die. Unfortunately our law does not give me that option, but the law also does not command that I love her as I would a son."

How could she turn her daughter over to another woman, allow another to suckle her, to teach her, to raise her? "But, Ba'ali—"

"Do not argue with me." His voice was low, each word pronounced distinctly and with malice.

Yana dropped to her knees, her hands folded in front of her chest. She drew in a deep breath, studying his face. Dare she say one more word?

She had to try.

"Ba'ali, I do not mean to argue." She kept her voice as calm and reverent as possible. "But suckling can last for only two years. It does not have to be three, and it does not inhibit conceiving for the entire time."

Would he allow her this one small thing? To him a luxury, but to her, life itself.

He bent over her, silent, unmoving. "If you do not obey me in this I will have the nurse not only suckle the child but be responsible for it in total, so that your *only* obligation will be to carry my child."

"I simply wish to appeal to your goodness and to the generous spirit I have so often seen you show others. I *beg* you to give me one year with my daughter. Allow me to nourish her, to be her sole caretaker for twelve months."

He pursed his lips. Had she made a crack in his resolve?

"I will make a sacrifice in the temple every month—every day if you desire—and ask Adonai to grant me, grant us, a son."

He sniffed and looked at the wall above her head.

"Please, give me, give *Adonai* a chance," she whispered.

He returned his gaze to her, stared for several long moments.

He held up one finger. "One year. Be thankful for my generosity. *One* year. Not a day longer."

Yana pressed a hand against her belly and tried to calm her breathing.

Sarai lay on the bed, blissfully unaware of the importance of this day. Eighty days ago, she had entered the world. Tomorrow Yana would appear at the temple to offer her sacrifice as required after childbirth.

Alone.

Oded had gone to Petra, and no amount of pleading or tears had been able to keep him in Jerusalem, even for such a ritual as this.

Yana took a long, narrow section of pale indigo cloth and tied the ends together in a knot, pulling on the ends to ensure it would hold. She slipped it over her head and slid one arm through so it rested on one shoulder.

She picked up Sarai and kissed her cheek, then gently placed her in the sling with her head toward the knot. She breathed deeply once more and left the house for the bridge.

Pausing outside the gate, she raised her face to the late spring sun. Light and warmth flooded her body and lifted her spirit. For the last eighty days, she'd glimpsed the sun only from her tiny window.

On the other side of the bridge, she could see the last of the smoke from the morning sacrifice climb toward heaven.

The sweet aroma of frankincense, cassia, and cinnamon grew stronger as she neared the western gate. How much of that was from Oded's spices?

Temple guards nodded as she strode through the gate and into the Court of the Gentiles.

First she needed to purchase a lamb for the sacrifice. Smiling to show more confidence than she felt, she marched to the southern portico, lined with tables and small shops. She chose a dealer with several lambs, doves, and other animals in an enclosure behind him.

"I need to make a sacrifice. I need a yearling lamb and a dove."

He smiled too widely. "Of course, of course. I have many." He gestured to the reed cages behind him. "Would you like to choose, or shall I?"

"You do it."

He pointed to a lamb. "Four denarii."

This was just like the market. Basya's advice rang in her ears. *Don't let him charge you too much.* "Four? It should be three."

The man, portly and bald, looked down on her as if correcting a small child. "And how would a woman know such things? The cost is four."

She lifted her chin. "My ba'al is Oded, who supplies the temple with spices for the holy incense. I know *such things.*"

The smile faded. He snatched the coins from her outstretched hand and shoved them into his sash. He selected a lamb and led it to her then handed her the rope along with a dove in a sack.

"Thank you." Once she entered the Court of Women, she blew out a sigh of relief.

A young priest met her at the Gate of Nicanor, which led into the Court of the Israelites. "Are you here to offer a sacrifice?"

She nodded as she moved the sling so he could see the babe. "For my purification."

He shifted his weight to look behind her. "And your ba'al?"

Her ears burned. "He is not here. I understood it was not required."

"It's not required, but—" Her face must have reflected her embarrassment, as he quieted and cleared his throat, then offered a genuine smile. "We shall offer the lamb first, as a burnt offering unto Adonai." He glanced at the animal. "You purchased it here?"

She nodded.

"Then it has been inspected and declared clean already." His voice was gentle and calmed her worries. "Now place your hand on its head. By so doing, your sins and unholiness are transferred."

Yana did as instructed. The wool on the lamb's head was softer than she'd imagined, and its little ears moved back and forth.

The priest took the rope from her and climbed the fifteen steps through the gate and into the priests' court, the yearling scurrying along behind.

Yana cringed as she heard the lamb's bleat stop suddenly. She stood on her toes in order to glimpse the altar.

The young man dipped his fingers into a bowl of blood, smearing it on each of the four horns of the altar. Other priests climbed the ramp to lay pieces of the slain lamb on the fire. The scent of burning flesh reached her before she saw the smoke wafting from the altar.

The young man reappeared. "And the dove?"

She held up the bag, the bird inside flapping its wings.

The priest reached inside and pulled out the bird. Holding it in the palm of one hand, he placed his thumbnail against the bird's neck. He pushed against the neck, snapping the windpipe but leaving the head attached to its body, limply hanging to the side.

Yana shivered, gulping back down the morning's food.

Once again he approached the altar and held the bird upside down, blood draining onto the altar from the bird's open mouth. The dove's tiny body would be roasted and the priests would later eat it.

She turned to go, her part completed.

Had her sacrifice pleased Adonai?

How would she know?

CHAPTER THIRTEEN

A person's wisdom yields patience;
it is to one's glory to overlook an offense.
~ Proverbs 19:11 ~

Month of Sivan
Late Spring, AD 32
Bethany, Judea

No matter how many times Yana entered the village of Bethany, her heart swelled with thankfulness. Since she had moved away, her appreciation had only increased. She was grateful to Adonai that she'd grown up around so many good and loving people.

She readjusted the sling that held Sarai close to her chest. The babe had grown rapidly in the past three months. She cooed, held Yana's gaze, slept for most of the night. Thank Adonai. There had been times when she didn't sleep for more than a few hours at a time, when Yana had almost wished she'd accepted Oded's offer of a wet nurse.

Almost.

Miriam reached the courtyard gate before Diana did. "Is this your baby?"

Yana could feel the smile that spread across her face. She pulled the sling over her head with one hand while the other supported the infant. "Yes. This is Sarai."

Miriam's hands were around the baby before Yana had her fully free of the layers of cloth. "Sarai! What a fitting name. You are beautiful! Just like your imma."

Sarai smiled and wriggled her hands.

"She likes me!" Miriam giggled.

Yana laughed with her. "Who wouldn't? You are the happiest person I know. It spreads to everyone y—"

A squeal interrupted her.

"The baby!" Marta drew near and took the baby from Miriam.

Yana chuckled softly. The only time she would hold Sarai today was when she was suckling.

"Shalom, Diana. We're so happy you could accompany Yana here." Simeon neared them and gave Yana a quick hug before stealing the babe from his daughters. "Keep an eye on that baby or you may lose her. We were wondering when we'd see this little one. We'd heard you had a girl but that was all."

"It's hard to get here. Oded doesn't like it when I'm gone." No need to tell them he didn't talk to her even when she *was* home.

Yana and Diana followed the trio into Simeon's house to the open-air common room, where she sat on one of the many colorful cushions scattered on the floor.

Simeon lowered himself to the cushion beside her, Sarai in his arms. "It's been a long time since I've held a baby. I know I'm biased, but she is the most adorable child ever."

"You are biased." Yana laughed. "And correct."

Miriam and Marta hurried back and forth from broadroom to table, setting out bowls and platters and baskets.

"How many people are you feeding?" Yana asked as Miriam set out one more basket.

Miriam smiled. "Just us." She looked at the table. "It was a good harvest."

Yana had forgotten what it was like to wait and see if the harvest would produce enough to keep them though the rainy season. She neither shopped nor cooked. Food just appeared on their table.

Miriam brightened. "Ezi was here a couple of months ago. He brought the teacher he's been traveling with—a man from Nazareth." The words tumbled quickly from her mouth. "We've met him and he speaks of Adonai as his abba. He also talks constantly about his abba's kingdom, so many think he is the promised Messiah who has come to overthrow the Romans."

"I'm not so sure he intends to do that," said Simeon. He carefully lifted Sarai up to face him. "Just beautiful, Yana." The sleeve of his cloak slid to his elbows.

Yana caught her breath. Several small white dots marked his arms.

"Uncle... What happened?"

He barely glanced at his skin. "The priest said it was all right. I go back in two weeks."

"You went to the temple?"

"As required." He set Sarai in Yana's lap. "I am fine, Yana. Nothing bad will happen to me."

She forced a smile.

"Adonai will work it out."

She nodded. That's what everyone said about her marriage to Oded.

That didn't work out either.

Month of Sivan

Late Spring, AD 32

Jerusalem, Judea

Yana adjusted the cloth holding Sarai as she climbed the narrow street to Oded's house. Diana followed behind with a small sack of yesterday's flatbread and goat cheese, which Marta had insisted they take.

They'd talked over the fire late into the night. Since Oded was in Ein Gedi, Yana decided to remain in Bethany overnight. She rose with the sun, nursed Sarai, and they headed for home, skipping the morning meal.

Diana held the door when they arrived home.

Yana slipped the sling over her head. Diana took it and began folding it while Yana settled Sarai in her arms.

Heavy footsteps sounded on the stairs behind her. "Eliyanah!"

Oded's rumbling voice behind her sent a chill through Yana's body from the blue scarf on her head to her dusty sandals. He was home? He was supposed to be at his desert groves, tending to his precious balsam trees.

Diana cringed and looked at the floor.

Yana closed her eyes and whispered a prayer before turning to face Oded.

Oded snapped his fingers at Diana. She scurried close, almost shaking.

"Take the baby."

Yana's knees buckled. Her chest constricted as Diana took her baby from her. From the corner of her eye, Yana could see him fisting and unfisting his hands as he waited.

What could she possibly have done to anger him so? She froze her face into a mask as he neared her.

"Where have you been?"

"I went to Bethany to show my family the baby. They hadn't seen her yet and—"

Oded glared at her. "I want you here when I return."

She bowed her head. "I beg your forgiveness, Ba'ali. I didn't know you would be returning so soon. When you go to your fields, you are always gone for at least five days."

He circled her slowly, his feet pounding the tiles in a haunting rhythm. "And since this is only the third day you thought it safe to go wherever you wanted to go, with whomever you wanted to go, to do who knows what?"

"I only went to show my cousins my daughter." She raised her head. "The law says that I have a right to visit my family."

He stopped before her, less than an arm's length away. "How would you, a mere woman, have any idea what the law says?"

She didn't dare tell him Simeon taught her about the law.

"You don't, do you? Only bits and pieces you think will benefit you. So I'm sure you don't know the law also says that you are to obey your husband. And I want you here when I am here."

"How am I to know when you will return?"

"That is not my problem."

"But this isn't fair. If I don't know when you'll be home, there is no way I can ever go to visit my family, and you can't keep me from visiting my family."

He leaned near, his face almost touching hers. "I can do whatever I wish. I am the ba'al."

"I don't know why you even care where I am. You only call for me in the middle of the night and then only for one week a month. The rest of the time I am invisible to you."

She saw only a flash of white linen and heard a sharp smack before the right side of her face exploded in pain. She stumbled several steps before she righted herself.

Diana stood huddled in the corner, Sarai held close to her chest, her eyes as big as fresh figs, her body trembling.

Yana smoothed her tunic and tucked her hair under her scarf before she turned around and brought her gaze back to Oded.

He pointed one long finger at her. "Do not ever contradict me." His voice was low, almost soft.

She preferred it when he yelled.

"You have one job—to produce a son. When and if you do that, you can have more freedom. Until then, you obey my every wish." He disappeared into his office.

Perching on the edge of a couch in the women's room, Yana flinched when a wet cloth touched her lip.

"I'm sorry. I know that hurts." Basya winced. Pink ripples of blood dissipated as she dipped the cloth into a bowl of water once more.

Yana ran her tongue over her lip, already swollen to twice its size. The tender flesh oozed blood, and the iron taste now coated her mouth. The inside of her cheek was cut from where it had smashed against her teeth.

The feel of the back of Oded's hand lingered. How could he do this?

Yes, she was his wife, and yes, he could control her every move. Under the law, she belonged to him every bit as much as his house, his fine robes.

His precious spices.

"I'm afraid it will take several days for the swelling to go down." Basya smiled weakly. "My brother was hit often when we were growing up. I used to tend his wounds too."

"Who struck him?"

Basya chuckled. "Other boys. Just playing too hard. He left his mark on them as well." She picked up the bowl and rested it against her hip. "I'll get some honey and make you some thyme tea for the pain." She left, gently closing the door behind her.

Yana fell back against the couch. She rubbed her cheek. She would have a dark blue bruise by tomorrow.

A soft knock sounded at the door. She rose to answer it and found Xander on the other side, a tray in his hands.

He glanced at her and then dropped his eyes. "I brought you something to eat—"

"Thank you, but I don't think I could eat anything now." She stepped back to close the door, but he stuck out a foot to hold it open.

"I know," he said, his voice firm but gentle. A soft color appeared on his cheeks and he raised his gaze to meet hers. "I've had many split lips. I know how painful they are. But you have to eat, and Diana said you haven't yet eaten today." He placed one hand under the tray, and with the other pointed at various dishes as he spoke. "I mashed up some fruit and peeled the crust from some bread. There is also some luke-warm soup."

Warmth spread over her face. How long had it been since someone cared for her in such a way? A way that required thought, sacrifice, and a knowledge of her needs?

She couldn't remember the last time.

"Th-thank you." She stared at him. His eyes reminded her of Ezi. Xander's were a gray-blue, not dark, but they held the same softness and compassion.

She longed for more of it.

He broke his gaze and pushed the tray toward her. "I should leave."

"Yes. Thank you again."

Xander turned to go but halted and faced her. "Try a paste of turmeric. It'll keep fever from setting in."

He strode quickly from the door.

Basya passed him as she returned. She narrowed her eyes and placed her fists on her hips. "He wasn't in here, was he?"

Yana placed the tray on the small table and collapsed again onto the couch. "Of course not."

"Because he can't come in here. You know that."

She looked up to meet Basya's gaze. "I do know that. And so does he. And he didn't."

"Then why was he at the door?"

Yana gestured to the tray. "He brought something he thought I would be able to eat."

"That's not his place. He should have sent his sister."

"Perhaps his sister never got hit in the mouth. She doesn't know what it feels like, and neither do you." Yana pulled her legs up onto the couch and rolled to face the wall. She closed her eyes. She was not going to discuss this with Basya.

"You're right," whispered Basya. "I don't know how it feels. I'm really sorry that you do. And I'm sorry that I don't know what to do to help you."

Yana sighed. None of this was Basya's fault. But Basya was adored by her husband. She'd given him two sons. And it seemed as though Elon would always love her, sons or not.

Yana had no idea how that felt. Oded had made it clear he'd married her only for an heir.

She was trapped here, in this house, in this life, forever.

Unloved. Unnoticed.

CHAPTER FOURTEEN

A cheerful heart is good medicine,
but a crushed spirit dries up the bones.
~ Proverbs 17:22 ~

Month of Tammuz
Early Summer, AD 32
Jerusalem, Judea

Yana held Sarai close as she suckled. The setting sun shot its last warm rays through the small window, bathing the babe in golden light.

Secluded in her room, shielded from the bustle of the house, Yana drew strength from these precious times when nothing else in the world mattered except for nurturing Sarai.

Not Oded. Not the lack of a son. Not being unloved.

All that was important was Sarai.

Sarai pulled away, eyes closed, a droplet of milk on her lower lip. She rested her head on Yana's breast, asleep.

Yana laid her on the bed and then sat beside her. She draped a light blanket over her. Would this tiny girl have a better life than Yana did? *Adonai, protect her.*

The door opened without a knock, and an older woman stepped inside. She had a kind face and wore an undyed wool tunic and headscarf. A basket hung from her arm.

Yana straightened and adjusted her tunic. Why was this woman in her room?

"I am Dalya, the wet nurse Oded sent."

Though her voice was pleasant enough, Yana's blood ran cold. She swallowed the scream that threatened to escape. There wasn't supposed to be a nurse for several months. With her hand protectively on Sarai's little body, she shook her head. "No, not yet."

Oded wouldn't do this.

Would he?

"I wasn't expecting you for many months."

The woman raised a brow. "I'm sure you're mistaken."

Yana closed the distance between them, tamping down her anger. "No, we talked about this. He said no nurse for a year."

Dalya stood firm. "Your ba'al contacted me this afternoon and instructed me to come to the house. He directed me to your chamber and told me to come up here."

"I'll see about this." Yana raced from her room, hurried down the steps and across the atrium, then burst into Oded's workroom.

He stood at a table, a large spoon in one hand and a bowl of ground spice in the other. A pair of matching bronze oil lamps cast flickering shadows over several bowls of spices that covered the table, and various sizes of alabaster jars like the one Ezi had given her sat on another. Shelves full of boxes and jars and small pouches lined the far wall.

He looked up from the table and raised a brow. "Is there a reason you have entered my room without permission?"

She drew in a deep breath, inhaling the strong aroma of frankincense. "There is a woman upstairs who claims to be the wet nurse you hired."

"Ah, yes. I spoke to her earlier."

"You gave me a year. It has not even been three months."

"She has an excellent reputation. I heard she'd become available, and if I did not hire her now, she would end up elsewhere for perhaps many years. Also, I have decided I can no longer wait that long. I need a son now." He dipped the spoon once again into the bowl. To him, the subject was obviously closed.

"But you promised." Yana did her best to keep the panic from her voice.

"I changed my mind." He moved to the shelves and selected a deep red pouch.

Her mind spun. What could she do to stop this? How could she give him what he wanted yet not lose what she had?

An idea struck her. "What if we both feed her?"

He turned around. "What? How would that work?"

"I will feed her first thing in the morning and before she goes to sleep, and any other time she awakens at night. The nurse can feed her during the day. That would be equal to what I would do more than a year from now. I should be able to conceive."

He pursed his lips. "I don't know...."

She took a step nearer. "You have always been an honorable man. Please keep the promise you made to me."

He thought a moment, crossing his arms. "The child will remain with the nurse at night so you are free to come to me. You may tend to her during the day."

Soon the babe would sleep all night, so perhaps this would be a better arrangement anyway. "Yes, Ba'ali."

He held up one finger. "You have until one year from her birth. In the meantime, we begin trying immediately."

"Yes, Ba'ali." She slunk from his room.

Until now, in the dark, lonely nights, she'd at least been able to thank Adonai for giving her a child. She could pull Sarai close and feel her breathing. Inhale her soft scent. Kiss her forehead.

Now there would only be a string of lonely hours, night after night, broken only by the times she was called to him for affectionless, wordless duty.

She tried to remember what Uncle Simeon had said.

"He will rejoice over you with singing."

But no matter how hard she tried, she could not hear Him.

Month of Tammuz
Early Summer, AD 32
Bethany, Judea

The sounds of giggles and birdsong filled the air. A gentle breeze carried the scent of ripening almond and grape blossoms. Towering date palms offered shade as the young women scrubbed the dwindling pile of dirty clothing. As Yana knelt on the bank with Miriam, washing tunics and blankets from the bet, it was almost as if she had never left. Why couldn't she have stayed here instead of living in a city made of cold, lifeless stone?

But then she wouldn't have Sarai. And even with Dalya's hovering, watching, taking note of everything so she could tell Oded upon his return, it was worth it.

Yana dunked a tunic and then wrung it out. She shook it and examined it for any remaining stains or spots. Satisfied it was clean, she rose and draped it over a nearby broom bush to dry.

Miriam joined her to spread another garment on the other side of the greenery. "Done. I'm hungry."

"You're always hungry." Yana smiled over the bush at her. "Like Sarai."

"True." Miriam laughed then grabbed their empty baskets and headed for the house. "Marta should have something for us to eat by now."

This time Dalya had come with her. She missed Diana's ready smile and bright face. But Oded had undoubtedly instructed Dalya to keep watch over Yana and most likely to report back to him as well.

Yana crossed her arms over her full breasts and quickened her steps back to the house. A midday meal of bread, olive oil, and goat cheese awaited. Yana retrieved Sarai from the nurse and took a seat on a cushion. She reached for a piece of bread and dunked it in the oil as Sarai begin to suckle.

Marta popped a fat grape in her mouth. "This afternoon we can collect the first grapes and start drying them for raisins." She gestured to Yana. "If you can stay that long."

Yana glanced at Dalya, who gave her a slight nod. "I can stay. I need to be home for the evening meal, though."

After they had finished eating, Yana laid a satisfied and sleepy Sarai on one of the beds for a nap. Dalya took a seat on the floor and pulled out a spindle and wool.

Though the sun was at its highest point, Yana had not yet seen her uncle. "Where is Uncle Simeon? I thought he'd be back by now."

Miriam paled. "I thought Marta told you."

Yana's stomach somersaulted. "Told me what?"

"He had to see the priest again. The spots on his arms were growing bigger, and…" Miriam's voice broke.

Miriam put a hand on Yana's arm. "The priest decided he had to be kept apart from everyone for seven days, so they are keeping him in a house in the lower city near the temple. On the seventh day, he will be examined again. If the priest decides the disease has not spread, Abba will be isolated seven days more."

"And then what?"

"The priest will examine him again on the seventh day, and if the disease has still not spread, the priest will pronounce him clean. But if it has…"

"It is *tsara'at*." Yana felt sick. She'd lost so many people already—would she lose Uncle Simeon as well?

"Come. If Abba returns and we have let the grapes wither on the vine, we'll be in trouble." Miriam chuckled weakly.

Yana pulled one plump grape after another from the vine, dropping them into a wide, shallow basket. Her thoughts kept returning to Simeon.

Miriam leaned near. "How did you get away, anyway? I thought he said you had to be there when he was."

"He relented a little. When he goes to Petra I can come if I ask him first, but not too often."

"How often is too often?"

"I'm not really sure." She swallowed. "But I may not be able to come for a while."

Miriam pouted. "Why not?"

"I think I am once again with child."

Miriam wrapped her in a hug. "Some good news for a change."

"It's still quite early. We'll see. If I can give him a son, then maybe..." The idea was too wonderful to hope for.

"Is he still distant?"

Distant didn't begin to describe his neglect. "I don't know how much longer I can continue. He's gone most of the time, and when he's home he never speaks to me. He's made it clear he married me for only one reason."

Her cousin shrugged. "What choice do you have?"

"None, I suppose. He's told me he will never divorce me."

"You can go to the priests, if you have a good reason."

"His imma is the daughter of a priest in the high court. I would never win." She stuffed a grape in her mouth. "The only joy in my life is Sarai, and he has taken her away from me for half the time."

"What?" Miriam stopped plucking grapes and stared at her.

"I can hold and see her only during the day. I'm supposed to have her all day, but Dalya feeds her as soon as she wakes and takes her back before she sleeps. He not only wants to limit my suckling her, he wants me free at night to go to him whenever he summons me."

Miriam's eyes misted. "Oh, Yana. I'm so sorry."

"If I'd known this, I would have taken the vow of the Essenes as you did."

"The celibate life is not perfect either, Yana. Every life has its challenges."

"And are you struck when you displease those around you? Is your every move controlled? Do you wear what others wish you to wear, eat what they desire?"

"No, I don't." Miriam returned her attention to the vines.

Yana squeezed her hand. "I'm sorry. This is not your fault. I know you dreamed of marriage as we all did."

She nodded. "I did. But I'm happy now. I do regret I will never have children, never know the love of a man, but I am following the path Adonai has chosen for me. I know I am pleasing Him, so I am pleased."

"I'm trying to follow His will. But I cannot say I am happy."

If Adonai allowed a faithful and kind man such as Simeon to suffer, what chance did she have?

CHAPTER FIFTEEN

He heals the brokenhearted and binds up their wounds.
~ Psalm 147:3 ~

Month of Av
Midsummer, AD 32
Jerusalem, Judea

Yana paused in the upstairs hallway and looked out over Jerusalem. What little she could see of the lower market from here was quiet, even for a day when the craftsmen's stalls were unattended. The bridge was nearly devoid of people. The wealthy sent servants to do their bidding so they could remain in the shade of their houses.

But a lifetime in the village had taught her to love the sun, even in the heat of summer. Without sun, there would be no crops. No grain, no grapes, no melons. Life would cease.

She lifted her face to the cloudless sky, allowing the orb's light to bathe her skin. She should be out in the fields helping with the harvest, not confined to a house, invisible except at Oded's command. She should be laughing with Miriam and Marta, with the other villagers as they worked to gather a year's worth of food in a few months. She should be tending to the sick at the bet.

But what should be was not.

She placed a hand on her belly. *Adonai, please, grant me a son.* She was still too afraid to be excited, but it had been almost three months. Longer than the time she'd lost the first baby but still in the time of risk.

Though he'd said nothing, Oded *had* to know she was with child. Exactly *how* he knew, she'd never been able to figure out, but he'd known the first time that she'd lost the baby before she'd even had a chance to tell him she was pregnant.

He'd not come home at the time she could conceive as he had every other month—further proof he already knew. In fact, he'd been gone longer than usual. It seemed that now that she was again carrying his child, he had no need to ever talk to her again.

The ache of loneliness had become her only companion.

She continued down the hall and descended the stone steps then turned to go to the women's room. Everyone else was gone, but she might as well continue to work on the wool blanket she'd started. She'd given the first one she made to the bet, since Oded refused to let her wrap Sarai in it. Since then she'd made and delivered several more. The one thing she could do to feel useful.

She jumped at the sight of Basya sitting on a Roman couch spinning yarn. "I didn't know you were here. I thought you'd be with Naomi at her abba's."

Basya shrugged. "He doesn't notice whether I'm there or not. He only cares about the boys, so I decided I'd just stay here this week. Besides, he wanted to take them to the temple, so I'd end up waiting there alone anyway."

"I'm sorry."

Yana headed for the loom leaning against the far wall, but a gasp from Basya interrupted her. She whirled around. "What's wrong? Are you all right?"

Basya's face had lost its color. "Yana, I'm so sorry...."

"What?"

One hand clapped over her mouth, Basya gestured to Yana's tunic.

Yana looked down but saw nothing. She rubbed her hands down the fabric and looked up to Basya, who spun one finger in a circle.

Yana twisted her head to check the back of her tunic and froze.

Not again.

How had she felt nothing? Nausea crept up her throat like a lizard crawling up a rock. She gulped and swallowed hard.

Adonai, please don't do this. She hurried to the lowest floor, every step another frantic prayer. *Please, please, please. Please let it stop.*

She removed her tunic and undergarments. The bleeding did not stop. She slid down the wall to the floor and placed her head in her hands, her arms on her knees.

Basya knocked softly.

She remained silent, distrusting her voice.

"Yana, it's me. I brought you fresh clothes…and some clean cloths for…"

She'd grown to hate the cloths she used every month. They'd become a tangible reminder of her failure to conceive.

"Just leave them."

"All right." A pause. "Yana, I'm so sorry."

Finally, footsteps leading away.

How could Adonai let her lose another baby? Didn't He know what it meant to her? To Oded? And how would she tell him?

A tear landed on her lips and she licked it away. The taste of salt lingered on her tongue. It was a taste she was getting far too used to.

Yana lay in her bed, numb. She could summon no more tears.

She'd cried them all.

All day, she'd remained in her room, fighting the cramping, the ache, the despair. Dalya had kept Sarai with her.

The events of this morning hovered in the back of her mind, refusing to fade. Any other thought was soon crowded out by the enormity of yet another loss.

Three times she'd been with child.

Only one baby.

Compared to the number who died before their first year, those results weren't bad. For her. For most women.

For Oded, they were unacceptable. Deplorable. Inexcusable.

Night was falling and stars were emerging in the inky black sky. Her belly ached, but was it because she was hungry or because of the chaos in her womb as another new life slowly slipped away?

A knock sounded. Probably Diana, bringing food. Such a sweet girl.

Yana swung her legs over the edge of the bed and sat a moment until the dizziness stopped. She rose and answered the door.

Diana waited on the other side, but she carried no platter. Her eyes were red and swollen. She shifted her weight, wringing her hands. "I fear I must ask for your pardon."

Pardon? "For what? You've always been quite attentive."

She stared at the floor. "I have betrayed you."

"How could you possibly betray me? And to whom?"

Diana looked up, her mouth quivering as she unsuccessfully tried to form words.

"Why don't you come sit down?"

The girl nodded and followed Yana into her chamber, eyes brimming with tears. She grabbed a stool and dragged it near the bed, then lowered herself onto it, her breath shaky. "When you first arrived, I was ordered to tell the ba'al everything I came to know about you."

Kneeling before her, Yana waved a hand. "He already knows everything. That is not betrayal."

"No, I mean, I wash the clothes...*everyone's* clothes." She fixed her gaze on Yana, trying to avoid explaining herself.

It took several long moments before she understood Diana's meaning.

"Oh, you mean whenever… So that's how he knows when I'm once again not pregnant. And how he knew I was."

How disgustingly sneaky.

Diana slid to the floor and bowed at Yana's feet. "I'm so sorry," she choked out. "He threatened to beat me. He did once—I was afraid it would happen again. But instead of protecting myself, I've put you in danger."

Yana hooked a finger under Diana's chin and raised her head to face her. "This isn't your fault. You didn't tell him anything he wouldn't have found out within days anyway."

"I know he's threatened to send you away."

"And you've done nothing to cause that." Yana tipped her head. "Why tell me this now?"

"I know you are no longer pregnant. And if I tell him, he will… I could wait a few days to tell him, if you want some time to prepare." She looked up expectantly, as if Yana could come up with something—anything—Diana could do to stop the consequences of her actions from hurting Yana too much.

But it wasn't Diana's fault. Oded always left a swath of destruction, affecting everyone sooner or later.

Yana pondered the offer. It would be nice to have a few days to mourn her loss before facing Oded's anger, but in the end, it would be the same. "You can tell him whenever he returns."

Diana grimaced. "When he's gone he expects a messenger to be sent. They can reach him by camel in hours when he is at Ein Gedi."

"Send the messenger in the morning."

Diana threw her arms around Yana. "I'm so sorry."

Yana pulled her close. "You've nothing to be sorry for."

No one could defy Oded for long.

Yana's thumbnail was chewed down to the skin. Alone in her chamber, she'd been waiting since daybreak for news of the ba'al's return. The messenger had gone and returned, but there was no sign of Oded, and the messenger had no news of his intentions.

He usually traveled at night. Perhaps he was waiting for the cooler air or finishing up business at his groves and would arrive tomorrow morning.

A night of rest would be welcome. The tension of hours of waiting had drained her muscles of their strength. She stretched her arms and legs, arched her back. She hadn't realized how exhausted she was.

She had just drifted off to sleep when an insistent pounding on her door awoke her.

Xander waited on the other side. "He...he wishes to see you."

There would be no rest tonight. "Thank you for telling me."

"I believe he is angry."

Of course he is. Why else would he want to see me in the daytime? "I'm sure he is." She stepped back inside and grabbed her cloak.

Xander's face clouded. "He should not treat you this way. There is no need for a husband to hit his wife."

She shrugged into the garment. "Diana told me he hit her once."

His mouth fell open. "*Hit* her? He nearly killed her. She didn't get out of bed for four days."

Yana's hand went to her throat. "I had no idea it was so bad."

"She spilled a drink on him."

"What?"

"She spilled pomegranate juice on him. That's why he struck her."

"For such a trivial offense?"

"He rarely needs a reason."

The compassion on his face warmed her heart. "I should go." She stepped into the hall and pulled the door shut behind her.

"Of course. Forgive me for delaying you." Xander stood aside to let her pass. For just a moment, his hand went to the small of her back as they headed for the stairs.

Standing outside Oded's workroom, Yana breathed in long and slow before she knocked softly.

"Come."

She opened the door and stepped toward him, stopping halfway between the door and his worktable.

"You failed again." His face was dark, his voice gruff.

"Yes, Ba'ali. I beg your forgiveness."

"This is because you go to Bethany too often."

What? How could he make that connection?

"From now on you will stay in Jerusalem, in this house. Dalya will inform me of your activities."

"Going to Bethany is not the reason I lost this baby."

He shrugged. "You can either stop visiting Bethany or stop nursing the girl. Your choice."

What kind of choice was that? Her daughter or her family? "Children are a gift from Adonai. Neither I nor you have any control over it."

"Nevertheless, I feel we need to do everything possible to allow you to deliver a son."

"Even if I do get pregnant again, I may not have a son."

He stepped closer. "If you do not produce a son next time, I will divorce you and keep your dowry."

She caught her breath. "The law says you can't keep it if you divorce me without cause. And not producing a son is not cause."

"And if I tell the priests you've been unfaithful, who do you think they'll believe? A common villager like you? Or the grandson of Benaiah ben Shammai?"

"You would lie to a priest to keep money you don't even need?"

"I will do what I must to produce an heir. If not by you, then by someone else."

And there it was. Her ultimatum.

Produce an heir or be shamed in front of all Jerusalem.

CHAPTER SIXTEEN

A friend loves at all times,
and a brother is born for a time of adversity.
~ Proverbs 17:17 ~

Month of Elul
Late Summer, AD 32
Jerusalem, Judea

Yana laughed as Sarai crawled around the women's room. Her skill at moving on hands and feet had blossomed in just the last week. Both mother and child looked up when a knock sounded on the door.

Xander waited, avoiding looking directly at her. "A man came to the gate.... He was a messenger from Bethany."

"From Bethany?" Who would be sending her a message from Bethany? They didn't know she wouldn't be returning soon, so what couldn't wait? "What happened? Is someone hurt? Ill?" Realization dawned, and her chest constricted. "Is it Simeon?"

Xander looked up. "He's quite ill. His daughters say you should come as quickly as possible. He has..." He furrowed his brows. "What did he call it...? Zar..."

"Tsara'at?"

"Yes."

Her heart nearly stopped. *No. Not Simeon.* Simeon was the most devout man she knew. He prayed about everything. He'd spent his life caring for others, leading the village with compassion and love.

Now he was the one who needed care.

"I have to go to him."

Xander jerked a thumb over his shoulder. "But Oded—"

"I'll have to change his mind." She brushed past Xander and hurried across the atrium to his door. She almost pushed her way in, but the last time she'd done that he'd become angry. She needed him calm. Reasonable.

She blew out a short breath and knocked gently.

"Come."

She opened the door but went no farther than the threshold. "Ba'ali, I've come to ask you to grant me a request."

"What is it?"

"It's extremely important to me. You remember my uncle Simeon, in Bethany?"

"Of course."

"He's quite ill. I need to go see him."

He threw her a quick side glance. "You just returned from Bethany."

"Two months ago!" She breathed deeply, trying to calm herself. "A messenger just arrived. He's grown much worse."

"If he is ill, then I don't want you or the baby around him."

She stepped toward him, her hands clasped at her chest. "Please, Ba'ali. He's my uncle. More like my abba, really."

"I told you, no. You stay here until you give me a son." His tone said the matter was closed.

"But—"

He glared. "No."

"What if it were your abba?"

"I'm not the one trying to get pregnant."

"I beg you—" She stepped just inside his door.

"Why are you so insistent?" He sneered. "Perhaps there is another reason you are so anxious to go to Bethany so often."

She threw her hands in the air. "What other reason could I have? This is my family."

He neared her. "What about that *child* you wanted to marry? Simeon's son, was it not?"

"He left. He's not even there anymore. I haven't seen him since before the wedding."

"Even if I believed you, which I don't, you don't think he will return if his abba is ill? You want to go and you're not even his daughter. Surely his son would want to be there even more than you do."

She huffed. "I don't even know if anyone knows where he is to get word to him."

"I doubt that."

"Ba'ali, I just want to see my uncle before—"

"You shall remain here." He turned his back on her.

Yana waited until she left his presence before allowing the tears to flow.

Yana stared at the ceiling, unable to enjoy the oblivion of sleep.

Adonai, take care of Simeon. If I can't see him, then...

Then what? He could live for years in the caves. Or die tomorrow. Tsara'at was notoriously unpredictable.

She could just slip out. Wait until night fell, until all were asleep. Through the front gate, to the lower market road, past the city gate.

That would be outrageously foolish, far too dangerous. Bandits, wild animals, dishonorable men... And what would Oded do to her on her return?

Maybe she wouldn't return. She could stay in Bethany. Live happily with Sarai... But Oded would surely come after her.

She knew very well she wouldn't do anything. She'd just stay here and hope for the best, pray that someday she could see Simeon again.

But when? After she finally conceived and bore a son? What if she had another daughter?

Then he'd divorce her and that would solve all her problems.

And create many more.

She groaned and rolled on her side.

Adonai, please don't let him die.

She draped an arm over her eyes, trying to shut out the dark thoughts.

The door opened, and Yana peeked from under her arm.

Naomi.

She pulled her arm back over her eyes, refusing to look at her.

"Yana?"

Go away.

"Yana, Oded will be leaving for Petra in the morning." She drew nearer. "I think you should go to Bethany."

Yana bolted upright, facing her. Was Naomi trying to get her in trouble? Get rid of her? "What did you say?"

Naomi sat on the bed beside her. "I think you should go. I lost my imma years ago. I wasn't able to see her before she died. I know…I know how important it is to say goodbye."

Yana shook her head. "But Oded—"

"I'll talk to Oded." She rose. "You can leave Sarai with Dalya, and Diana can accompany you. You and I both know it will do nothing to hurt your chances of conceiving."

Her offer seemed too good to be true. How did she even find out about Simeon? Surely Oded would never have told her. "Why are you doing this?"

"I told you. It's important to say goodbye."

Yana frowned.

Naomi stood. "I know you have little reason to trust me. But although I may have been overly critical of you, I have never betrayed you, or anyone for that matter."

That much was true.

Naomi left the room, softly closing the door as she did.

Yana lay back down, going over the conversation again and again in an attempt to determine Naomi's plan.

Should she go? She might as well try. What could happen?

Month of Elul
Late summer, AD 32
Bethany, Judea

As soon as they reached Simeon's house, Yana raced inside. "Marta! Miriam!" She and Diana raced from room to room searching for someone, anyone, who could point her to Simeon.

The bet. They would know.

A young woman exited from Yana's former house. "Are you looking for Miriam and Marta?"

Yana eyed her, but she had no time to consider why this woman was in her house. "Yes. Where are they?"

She gestured north, toward the Mount of Olives. "They went to the caves to care for their abba."

The caves? Her body shuddered uncontrollably. She put her hand to her mouth and felt the burning in the back of her throat.

Diana wrapped an arm around her waist.

"What…? Why? They didn't say anything about moving him to the caves. The message only said he'd grown worse."

The young woman shrugged. "I don't know."

Realization hit her like cold water in the face. *The message said I should come as soon as possible.* Marta obviously didn't want to say he was in the caves in case Oded intercepted it. And it had taken another day before Yana could arrive.

She was too late.

"You can probably catch up to them on the path."

She sprinted back up the village street toward the Mount of Olives, Diana hurrying to keep up. Gust billowed up around her, filling her mouth and causing her to cough.

At the end of the road, past the gate, she turned right toward the group of caves used by the village for burials. Years ago, lepers had moved into the caves. Here they were safe from spreading their ritual uncleanness but close enough so the villagers could leave food and clean clothes for them.

Ahead, faces down, shoulders hunched, Miriam and Marta walked toward her.

"Miriam!" Yana raced to her and threw her arms around her cousin, who retuned her fierce embrace. For one of the few times in her life, Miriam was not smiling.

"Yana, I'm so glad you've come," Marta said, eyes red. "I sent a message, but I wasn't sure you'd get it."

"I did. It just took me a day or two to be able to leave. But I'm here now. Where is he?"

"He's in the caves. I'm sorry we didn't tell you, but we were afraid—" Marta choked down a sob.

"You have nothing to apologize for. You had to do what's best."

"Best for whom?" Miriam's dark eyes flashed. "Best for *Abba* would be that we care for him at home, not shove him into a dark cave."

Marta placed a hand on her shoulder. "Miriam, you know the law as well as Abba. He can't stay at home."

"Come." Miriam grabbed Yana's hand. "I'll take you."

"Diana, you can stay with me while she sees him." Marta wrapped her arm around Diana's shoulder and continued her journey to the house.

"We're taking turns caring for him," said Miriam. "We grind the grain in the morning and make the bread. Then one of us goes to the bet and the other comes here. We've been trying to come later in the day because once we touch him, we can't do anything else until sundown since we're unclean."

Yana hadn't thought of that. If she touched him, she'd have to stay overnight since it would be unsafe to travel over the mount in the dark.

"Abba's more concerned about the people in the bet than he is for himself. He's always shooing us away, telling us to go see to them, saying he'll be fine here without us."

"That sounds like him." Sweet Uncle Simeon. He was always caring for others, thinking about others. That's what made him such a great leader. No one slipped by unnoticed. Everyone's needs were met somehow.

As they neared the caves, she heard a cry. "Unclean! Unclean!"

Simeon. She would know that voice anywhere.

A few steps closer allowed her to see him. Her heart shattered when she saw him dressed in rags.

Others came out of the cave, some who'd obviously been there for years. Hair hanging loose. Beards in need of a trim.

She'd always known about the lepers here. She'd even brought food out here and left it at the mouth of the caves so those inside could retrieve it. Bethany had always cared for the sick, including the lepers.

But one of her own family? Simeon?

Why Simeon?

She stepped closer. "Uncle, I came as soon as I could."

He flashed a reassuring smile. "I know you did. But, Yana, you should not be here."

"How can I not be here?" Tears rolled down her cheeks. How she wanted to hold him, let him know how much he was loved.

"You have a baby. You cannot risk becoming unclean."

"I know, but I had to see you."

"I know. And I'm truly glad you did. But I will be fine."

"How can you be fine? You're all alone."

"I'm not alone. There are nine or ten of us out here." He grinned.

"You know what I mean. You have no family with you, no one who loves you."

He looked up to the heavens for a long moment. "Remember the prophet Isaiah?"

She nodded.

"The Lord told him, 'So do not fear, for I am with you; do not be dismayed, for I am your God. I will strengthen you and help you; I will uphold you with my righteous right hand.'" He smiled. "The Lord is with me. I am never alone."

"If you say so." It was nice he could believe that, but she knew better.

"You cannot hear Him, can you?"

How did he know that? She shook her head.

A soft smile graced his face. "Then you are not listening."

Or maybe He just wasn't singing.

CHAPTER SEVENTEEN

He who is slow to anger is better than the mighty,
and he who rules his spirit, than he who captures a city.
~ Proverbs 16:32 ~

Month of Elul
Late Summer, AD 32
Jerusalem, Judea

The nurse had been instructed to report Yana's every movement to Oded, and unless Naomi had kept her promise to talk to him, there was no way he would let this go without punishment. Even if Naomi had discussed it, there was no guarantee he wouldn't simply change his mind. For the last four days all she could do was wait until he came home. She awakened early and slept little, wanting to be ready for the booming sound of his voice, the stomp of his sandals. It had been four days of waiting and wondering and fear.

Early in the morning of the fifth day, with the sun barely cresting the walls of the Temple Mount, the courtyard gate opened. Heavy footsteps sounded in the atrium and up the front stairs to Oded's room.

Yana could hear him stomping around in the room next to hers.

There was no way to tell whether it would happen now or later. If she were lucky he would sleep a while, perhaps bathe, before he talked to Dalya. Still, better to be ready than caught unaware.

Yana rose and dressed. She straightened up her chamber even though Diana would do it all again later. She arranged and rearranged the jars of oils and pots of ointments on her table—by size, then by color, then by scent.

The sun was high in the sky when someone finally came to her door to relay the summons.

Diana was nearly in tears herself and trembling. "I told him nothing, I promise you, but he knows. He knows you went to Bethany."

"I know you didn't tell him. He asked the nurse to keep track of my movements and report to him." Yana pulled her close. "Don't worry. I knew this might happen, but it was worth it."

"I will pray to the goddess for you." Diana wiped away tears. "You are very brave."

Yana certainly didn't feel brave. If Diana could hear Yana's heart pounding she would realize how terrified she was.

Oded waited for her in the center of the atrium, jaw clenched and hands closed into fists. He jerked his thumb toward his office. Yana obeyed, and Oded followed her.

He slammed the door closed and stalked to the other end of the room. "You deliberately defied me."

He was angrier than she expected. Had his imma not talked to him yet? "Naomi said I should go. She said she would talk to you about it."

"She did not talk to me about it, and as you can see, she is not here."

Her heart sank. Of course not. It was the second day of the week. Her knees began to buckle. Had Naomi lied to her? Or had she just not seen her son yet?

She thought quickly. "Perhaps we could wait until she returns from her abba's. Or send a messenger."

"We will not be waiting. We will not be sending anyone anywhere. *All* we will be doing is deciding what should happen to you for your deliberate disobedience." He took off his cloak and laid it over the table nearest him.

Panic began to rise in her. She tried to stuff it down. "Ba'ali, I am so sorry. I thought if I had Naomi's permission—"

"Now you know differently. I don't care if she gave you permission or not. It isn't hers to give. I am the ba'al in this house, and I make the decisions." He strode slowly near her. Would he slap her again? What could she say to stop him?

A loud knock on the door halted him.

"Not now," he growled.

The door opened and Naomi entered. Only she could have entered after his harsh words without serious consequences.

Oded looked past Yana at his imma, eyes narrowed. "I said *not now.*"

She came farther into the room, apparently unfazed by his command. "I heard you were in here with Yana. I wanted you to

162

know that I told her to go. I remember when Imma died...." Her face softened. "I thought she should see him before it was too late."

"Thank you, Imma. I understand."

"You will not hurt her then?"

"I said I understand."

Naomi eyed him, clearly not reassured.

Oded smiled and led her from the room.

Yana turned toward him. Had she escaped his wrath?

He scowled and came near her again, each step slow, deliberate. Menacing.

"Ba'ali, please try to understand. I had to see Simeon."

He closed the distance between them and grabbed her upper arms. He squeezed and lifted her up on her toes to bring her face close to his. "*I* do not have to understand anything. *You* have to obey. Do *you* understand?"

Fiery pain shot from her arms to her shoulders, to her hands. "You're hurting me. Please let me go."

He did as she asked and then drew his left hand up toward his right shoulder and backhanded her. She stumbled to the side, hitting the low stone table that sat in front of his couch. She tried to regain her balance and was nearly upright when he slapped her again. She fell onto the hard tile floor, striking her hip and her elbow.

He grabbed her by one arm and pulled her back to her feet. "*Now* do you understand?"

She managed to nod.

"If pain is the only thing that can teach you, then you shall have more." One more blow sent her to the floor. This time she didn't get up. She pulled her knees to her chest, wrapped her arms around her head, and waited for the next blow.

Yana awakened in her own bed, legs curled up to her chest. She vaguely remembered being helped up the stairs by Naomi and Basya.

Crowing roosters announced the dawn.

How long had she slept? The next morning? She had slept nearly a whole day?

She tried to roll onto her back and immediately regretted it. Piercing pain shot through her body.

Visions of Oded hitting her flashed through her mind.

She lifted an arm. Blue and yellow bruises adorned her skin where he had grabbed her. A bump protruded from above her ear from hitting the stone table. She rubbed her hip, aching from colliding with the table. She moved her jaw and winced. She could feel the swelling without even touching her face.

Groaning, she swung her legs over the side of the bed then slowly stood. With one palm on the wall to steady herself, she breathed through her nose until the room stopped spinning. She hobbled to the corner and looked in the polished brass mirror. Bruised cheek. Black eye. A small cut—likely from his signet ring—graced her chin.

Lowering herself to the stool, she reached for the brush. She slowly drew it through her long locks, every tangle pulling on the tender flesh of her scalp. She dribbled a few drops of vanilla-scented oil on the tip of a finger then gently dabbed it onto the cut, wincing at each touch.

Hugging the wall, she made her way to the door and then downstairs. Every step brought agony, and her breasts ached to feed Sarai. How long had it been? Yesterday, before Oded called for her. She headed for Dalya's room. No one responded to her knock. She gently pushed open the door.

No nurse. No Sarai. Where was everyone?

Her stomach rumbled. She'd had some bread and cheese yesterday morning before…before he came home. She'd eaten nothing else all day yesterday. No wonder she was hungry. She shuffled across the dining area and into the cooking space. Would there be anything she could eat in here? She touched her jaw and flinched. It would be difficult.

A loaf of fresh bread sat on the table. She ripped it in two and pulled apart some of the soft center then placed tiny pieces on her tongue. It didn't take long for her to gobble it down.

What else? She rummaged through baskets and boxes, trying to find anything soft enough to eat. She had selected a peach from a basket of fruit and was reaching for a knife when Xander walked in on her.

His face paled. The muscle in his jaw jumped.

"Where is my baby?"

"Oded and Elon went to Petra. Diana went with Basya, Naomi, and the boys to the market."

"And Sarai?"

"I think the nurse took her as well. It's such a nice day she wanted her to spend some time outside." He continued staring. His voice was flat.

Was he angry with her? She studied the floor. When he remained silent, unmoving, she headed for the door, leaving the fruit behind.

Xander's broad shoulders and crossed arms blocked the door.

She bounced her foot. What did he want? Why wouldn't he move? She took a step toward him, close enough to hear his quickened breath, smell the cloves on his hands, see the flecks of silver in his eyes.

"Don't go yet. Please." Her cheeks flamed as his eyes roamed over her face. He took in her black eye, purple cheek, the cut on her chin. His fingers hovered over her wounds. "I'm sorry. I feel like this is my fault."

"How could it be your fault?" Would her heart stop pounding if she backed away from him?

"I mentioned the message from Bethany to Naomi. She told you to go, and now…" He moved past her to wet a clean cloth with water from the cistern buried in the corner of the room. "I should have kept my mouth shut."

"You were trying to help. And it worked. I got to see him. Whatever happened, I deserve it. I went against his wishes." She shook her head. "I was not a good wife."

His eyes widened as he returned to her. He nearly laughed. "That's ridiculous! *He* is not a good husband."

She glanced at the door.

"Don't worry. No one else is home." He dabbed the cloth on her face. The water from the buried cistern was cold, and it felt good on her bruises. "No man should ever treat a woman this way." He gently pushed her hair back and drew the damp cloth over her forehead, her ears, and her jaw. He rubbed his thumb over her lips. One corner of his mouth turned up. "At least your lip didn't split open again."

His hands were soft and tender. He was so near she could feel his breath on her cheek. "If I could do anything about it, no one would ever touch you in anger again."

"Kiss me," she whispered. How long had it been since anyone had kissed her?

Ezi had stolen a few kisses before Simeon told her she would marry another. That was over two years ago.

"What?" His brow furrowed.

She shook her head. What a foolish idea. Shame washed over her, and she started to push past him.

He sidestepped to block her path. "Are you sure?" His low voice sent shivers down her spine.

"I'm sure."

"I don't want to hurt you."

"I don't care." She needed someone to show her she mattered, to prove she was desirable.

He leaned nearer and brushed his lips over hers. His lips were soft, his kiss gentle.

She pulled back and studied his face. Light skin. Dark hair and a smooth face. Gray eyes full of tenderness. She could so easily find herself in trouble. Xander was everything Oded was not. He was not Ezi, but he was kind and good and gentle. If she couldn't have Ezi, why couldn't she have been promised to someone like Xander?

The enormity of what she had done burst into her mind like a desert sunrise. "I should go."

Xander stepped back, giving her plenty of room to escape.

CHAPTER EIGHTEEN

Above all else, guard your heart,
for everything you do flows from it.
~ Proverbs 4:23 ~

Month of Tishri
Early Fall, AD 32
Jerusalem, Judea

The arrival of cooler weather before the rains started had prompted Oded to give a special treat to his family. He had taken Naomi, Elon, Basya, and the boys to the groves of Ein Gedi with him to celebrate the last day of Sukkot.

Yana, of course, had been instructed to remain at home lest she endanger any pregnancy that might have begun. It had been a long day.

Dalya had already taken Sarai from her for her final feeding. The night stretched out before her like an unending void.

She wasn't sleepy, but dawn was many hours away. How would she fill the time? Night after night until they returned? She could go to the women's room and weave. She did that almost every day.

She strolled into the cooking area. Oded had taken Sopha along as well to cook for them and Kronos to help with the shelters and baggage. She peered into the baskets, but nothing looked appetizing. She wasn't hungry anyway.

She glanced at the cistern where Xander had dipped the cloth he used to tend to her wounds. Where he… Yana touched her fingertips to her lips. Though it had happened two weeks ago, she could feel his kiss lingering, filling her heart with a fire she'd never experienced.

What if she went to see him? She halted as if she'd walked into a wall. Where had that thought come from?

Though Oded had made his feelings about her more than clear, Xander's were less certain. Still, he had at least kissed her.

Oded hadn't.

She chewed on her nails. What to do? Did she really want to share herself with another man?

It wasn't like she'd ever truly given herself to Oded. He took what he wanted and sent her away. Didn't she deserve to know the love of a man who truly cared for her? At least once?

She paced in the atrium, thinking, wondering, arguing with herself.

Adonai hadn't answered her prayers. Any of them. Not for Simeon, not about a husband, not for a son.

If He wasn't going to take care of her, she'd have to do it herself.

She found herself in front of Xander's room. Her heart beat against her chest, the sound pounding in her ears. Her fingers and toes tingled as if she'd been stung by honeybees. She could think of nothing except the feel of his lips on hers, the touch of his hands.

She rapped her fingertips on the closed door.

No answer.

Should she try again or just leave now, before she got into deeper trouble?

Xander opened the door. He stared at her, mouth open, saying nothing.

"I...I wanted to see you again."

He swallowed and ran his hands through his hair. His shoulders tensed.

Her cheeks burned and she dropped her gaze, resisting the urge to race up the stairs and shut herself in her chamber, never to come out again. How could she have been such a fool? He'd been avoiding her ever since that day. Refusing to look at her, leaving when she got anywhere near him. He wasn't interested in her after all.

Apparently no one was.

She'd spent weeks dreaming of his kiss—of another kiss, and he obviously regretted the first one. "I-I'm sorry. I misunderstood. I should go." She turned, but he reached for her, laying a hand gently on her upper arm—the same place Oded had bruised.

"Please stay." His voice was rough. "You didn't misunderstand."

She halted but didn't turn around.

He came up behind her, his other hand landing gently on her waist. His breath—as shallow and rapid as hers—caressed her neck. "I want you to stay," he whispered. "You have no idea how much I want you to stay. But..."

She turned in his arms, placing her hands on his chest. "But what?" She searched his eyes for any sign of what he meant, what he was thinking.

"You don't belong to me. You belong to another—"

"Who doesn't love me. Who cares for me not one iota. Who wants me only for what I can give to him while he gives nothing at all." Didn't Xander understand?

He shook his head slowly. "I know, but he is so very powerful. And angers so easily."

No one knew that better than she did. She placed a hand on his cheek. "I will die if I have to live like this," she whispered. "Even if it lasts only one night, I need to feel loved."

He drew in a sharp breath.

"Kiss me again."

A smile slowly blossomed. He bent his head but turned away from her mouth to kiss her neck.

Yana closed her eyes, relishing the feel of Xander's lips as he worked his way from below one ear to the other.

He pulled back and cupped her cheek with one hand, the other at the small of her back. "Has anyone ever told you how beautiful you are?"

Ezi did. Often. That felt like another life.

Xander covered her mouth with his own as he pulled her into his chamber. He spun her around, kicked the door shut, and backed her toward his bed.

She broke the kiss and raised one foot to slide it onto the bed behind her. She pulled her other leg up and sat on her knees facing him.

Xander knelt beside her. He wrapped her in his arms and pulled her close, and his lips hovered over her skin. He kissed her cheeks, her temples, her forehead, and finally touched his lips to hers.

The warmth of his touch flooded her body.

If only she could stay here forever, in his arms.

Yana awoke to Xander softly running his fingertips down her back, sending her heart racing. She rolled over to face him.

His face was a finger's breadth from hers.

She melted into his kiss. The feel of his body next to hers suffocated every other thought. Though she'd been married for nearly two years, she'd never been held like this, loved like this. No one had spoken to her with such tenderness, looked upon her as a priceless treasure.

It would likely never happen again. She cherished every moment, burning his scent, his touch, every look, and every whispered word into her memory. This memory would have to carry her through many long years of Oded's indifference.

A crashing sound registered vaguely.

Xander twisted to face the door.

Yana screamed as four men in white robes burst into the room. She scrambled backward on the bed.

One scribe grabbed Xander by the arm and pulled him to his feet. The man drove him backward and pinned him against the wall, his forearm against his throat.

Pain shot through her shoulder as another grasped Yana's hand and wrenched her off the stuffed mattress. She reached for her cloak but he ripped it from her hand, glaring at her with a smirk. "You shall come as you are, harlot."

She glanced at Xander. The fear that consumed her was reflected on his face. His eyes were wide, his chest heaving, his hands clenched with no one to strike.

"What about this one?" the man who held Xander spoke, but to whom? The others ignored him.

A man in a fine black robe entered the room. A striped black-and-white prayer shawl draped around his shoulders and reached his knees. Though his face was unwrinkled, his long gray beard belied his age. Hard eyes scanned the room, his gaze stopping on Yana. His upper lip curled and his nose wrinkled as if he could smell her sin.

Nausea bubbled up from her belly. Though the Pharisee kept his eyes on her face, his unmistakable disgust felt like a load of dung had been piled on her shoulders.

With no less disapproval, he turned his attention to Xander. "He is Greek, yes?"

One of those guarding him dropped his gaze down Xander's body. He sneered. "He is."

The Pharisee shrugged. "We can do nothing since we have no authority over him. Let his ba'al deal with him. Keep him here, away from her, until we are gone, then let him go."

Gone? Where were they going?

What would happen to Sarai?

Xander strained against his guards. "Where are you going? Where are you taking her?"

One of the men let loose a hard blow to his gut.

Xander doubled over, wheezing. "Leave...her...alone."

Even in his pain he tried to protect her. She whimpered. "Xander, don't," she whispered.

The Pharisee jerked his head toward the door. "Bring her."

One of the scribes pulled on her.

"Please, my cloak." She gestured at the garment on the floor, pleading with the man.

He scoffed and pulled on her arm.

"Hasn't she been humiliated enough? Let her have her cloak," said Xander.

His guard punched him in the ribs with a closed fist. Xander groaned and his knees buckled.

The guard who held her yanked on her arm. "Move. Now."

"Take care of Sarai!" Yana hunched her shoulders in a vain attempt to hide her body as the scribe dragged her out the door of Xander's chamber.

She looked across the atrium. Dalya, apparently roused by the noise, stood frowning in her doorway, holding Sarai. The babe stretched one tiny arm toward Yana, her face pinched in distress and confusion. The nurse took Sarai away and closed the door behind her.

The scribe dragged Yana across the atrium to the front gate, where the Pharisee waited, arms folded into the sleeves of his robe. He looked straight ahead, not at her.

One of the men who had held Xander scurried ahead and opened the gate, stepping back to allow the religious leader to precede him out of the house.

Yana was propelled down the street. As usual at this hour, the narrow alleys between the houses were empty, but in a few moments she would step onto Jerusalem's most prestigious street, the bridge from the upper city to the temple, with nowhere to hide.

CHAPTER NINETEEN

The teachers of the law and the Pharisees brought
in a woman caught in adultery.
They made her stand before the group and said to Jesus,
"Teacher, this woman was caught in the act of adultery."
~ John 8:3–4 ~

One arm over her chest, the other in the iron grip of the scribe, Yana tried desperately to keep up. Repeated stumbles left her knees and the tops of her feet nearly scraped raw. Cold morning air rushing over the bridge whipped her hair and stung her skin.

Wealthy women stared. Levites and scribes allowed their eyes to wander. Children giggled and pointed at the throng of men leading her, pulling her, dragging her like an animal.

Yana swallowed the sick taste that soured her mouth. "Where—where are you taking me?"

"You'll be taken to the temple, to the court of the Sanhedrin, where the priests will find you guilty since there are witnesses." The scribe's gravelly voice oozed hatred. "After that they will decide the punishment, which undoubtedly will mean you will be stoned."

Yana's heartbeat stuttered. Stoned to death? When was the last time someone was actually stoned for adultery? The worst punishment for infidelity that she knew of was to be stripped and sent from the husband's house, shame and guilt evident for all to see. She hadn't heard of even that happening in decades.

Adonai, help me, please.

Did she deserve His help? By her own actions she had brought this upon herself. She'd known the risk when she went to Xander, but she thought the worst that could happen was that Oded would divorce her. He may have insisted on the ordeal of bitter waters, but why bother waiting months when he could divorce her at his pleasure?

The dowry. This was all about the dowry.

Why couldn't she have had the attitude Simeon had even while he faced death? Even in the cave he had not questioned Adonai's care for him.

She continually questioned His love for her, and where had it gotten her?

At the end of the bridge, the group slowed. Ahead waited yet another man, his back to her. She'd guess a priest by his clothes.

He turned as they reached the end.

Benaiah.

Her stomach revolted, and she doubled over and retched. With little in her stomach, though, the painful heaves produced nothing.

The Pharisee joined Benaiah, and the scribes fell in line behind them as they continued to the temple.

The western gates of the temple loomed over them. Guards in long white robes and headwear opened them, and the scribes dragged her into the court of the Gentiles. Worshippers gasped, pointed, and snickered.

The group veered left toward the north wall of the Temple Mount.

Yana's stomach roiled. The Sanhedrin. The group of seventy-one met in a chamber with doors opening onto the temple grounds on one side and to the city on the other.

These men, who spent their days discussing and interpreting the smallest aspects of the law, would decide her fate. Men used to being obeyed, in control, separated from anything the least bit unholy. How could they possibly have any mercy for her, understand why she did such an unthinkable thing?

The man dragging her halted so suddenly she almost ran into him. Ahead of them the Pharisee huddled with Benaiah, staring south toward Solomon's Porch. A sly smile crossed his face.

They beckoned to the scribes.

Benaiah pointed toward the colonnaded porch on the southern edge of the temple. "I have a plan that will solve many problems."

Yana kept her eyes on the polished marble tiles cut into intricate geometric designs that made up the floor of the temple, but she kept her ears on the conversation between her captors.

"Why do you always want to complicate things?" She didn't have to see the Pharisee's face to know he was annoyed. "Solving one problem at a time is enough. And we have been paid—"

"Hush!" growled Benaiah. "This rabbi over there, he's the one who is promising the people a new kingdom, yes?"

"Yes."

"And we need a way to discredit him, yes?"

"We do." The Pharisee was growing impatient.

"He's over there at this very moment, telling the people what they want to hear."

Yana raised her head just enough to look through her lashes. Benaiah pointed to a growing crowd gathered around a rabbi on Solomon's Porch on the eastern side of the temple.

"And?" The Pharisee frowned.

"We take her to him, tell him she has been caught in the act of adultery," said Benaiah. "We ask him if we should stone her as the law requires. If he consents to our request to stone her, he will encourage the Jews to defy the Romans. However, if he refuses, he will make it clear to all that he does not support the Law of Moses."

The Pharisee smiled. "We rid the country of a dangerous traitor, and we secure our positions with both the people and with the Romans."

"And we still take care of *this* problem." He tilted his head toward her. "You should trust me more."

The Pharisee chuckled. "And either way, we have made it clear the rabbi is no friend of the Jewish people. Yeshua ben Yosef does not keep the law and cannot be hailed as the Messiah."

Yeshua ben Yosef? Just when she was hoping not going to the Sanhedrin meant she would avoid a stoning. Yeshua ben Yosef was the one who toppled the tables two years ago. With a *whip*. If he did that to money changers legally doing business, what would he do to her?

Benaiah began walking again, but instead of heading for the high court, they veered toward the famous portico. Just as the waters of the Jordan parted when the feet of the priests touched them, people made way for the honored men hustling a naked woman over holy ground.

Though it was still quite early, she could see the rabbi sitting on a low stool talking to a gathering crowd of men and women. Some sat, some stood, but all listened to every word he spoke as if it were delivered from the mouth of Adonai Himself. Yet from his dress—and the way her captors talked about him—he was not a priest, Pharisee, scribe, or even a Levite.

When they neared the portico, the scribe moved behind her. With one harsh hand on her bare shoulder, he shoved her between two of the massive columns.

Her knees hit the hard tile first. She avoided hitting her face by breaking her fall with her hands. She crossed her arms over her chest, crouching low, arms resting on her legs, trying to hide as much of her nakedness as possible.

Was she not to be tried? Or would she appear there after their test of the rabbi was completed? Would she still be stoned?

And the one thought that never left her—what would happen to Sarai?

Yana kept her head down. She could hear footsteps behind her as the rest of the men who had dragged her here, and more who had joined along the way, moved to stand around her and the rabbi. At last she saw Benaiah's sandals near her head, his black robe swirling about his ankles. She could feel his cold stare on the back of her neck.

Beyond the Court of the Gentiles, past the Court of Women, the Levites sang the psalms of the Hallel while the priests prepared the morning sacrifice. The scent of holy incense wafted through the courts. How much money had Oded made by selling the sacred ingredients at his inflated prices?

"Rabbi, this woman was caught in the act of adultery." Benaiah's voice was both condescending and patronizing at the same time. "In the Law, Moses commanded us to stone such women. What do *you* say?"

More footsteps. Not Benaiah's—his feet hadn't moved. Whose?

A woman's sandals came into Yana's field of view, and a soft cloak was gently draped over her unclothed body and tucked around her shoulders. A hand rested on her head for a fleeting moment.

Scoffs and huffs came from the men standing over her.

Yana stretched one arm to touch the feet of her unknown benefactor. She longed to look up to see who would have the courage to undo what the scribes had done, but she dared not. She tucked her arm back under her body, then stretched her fingers until she felt the fabric and held tight.

The crowd backed away, farther down the portico. Unwilling to be part of the Pharisee's scheme? Or just too timid?

She grasped at a morsel of courage and raised her head just enough to see the rabbi's face. Dark, wavy, unoiled hair just touched the neck of his cloak. His garments were not fine linen, as most learned men wore, but rough, undyed wool. The skin of his hands and feet suggested he was quite young, but his muscular forearms spoke of hard work. Most of the crowd she'd seen as she approached appeared older than he was, and the men who had brought her to him were most certainly his elders.

The rabbi bent over, one finger extended. He touched it to the cutwork tile, obscured by sandal prints after the crowds of the Feast of Sukkot had spent the last week walking on it. Carefully, unhurriedly, he guided his finger through the layer of dust.

The holy men shifted their weight and whispered among themselves.

"Why does he not answer?"

"The arrogance of this man. Who does he think he is?"

Benaiah spoke up again, his voice reflecting his growing irritation. "Rabbi, we require an answer."

The younger man remained quiet.

Yana studied the marks he made. The letters looked Hebrew, not Greek, but since she could read neither it mattered little.

"Rabbi." Benaiah raised his voice. "This woman was caught in the act of adultery. We bring her to you along with five witnesses. Moses commanded us to stone such women. What do you say?"

The man stilled his hand. He rested his arms on his knees and looked up at the witnesses.

His face was peaceful, gentle. Unaccusing. So unlike the cold, hard, condemning faces of the scribes surrounding her.

"If any of you is without sin, an unbiased witness as the Law of Moses requires, then you shall throw the first stone in punishment." His voice was softer than she expected, but somehow evidenced more authority than she'd have thought his years would command.

Heart beating wildly, Yana squeezed her eyes tight, awaiting the barrage of rocks that was surely to come since the rabbi had given his permission. Her breath was rapid and shallow, and the fingernails she had left cut into her palms.

Tension saturated the air more than the sacred spices. The sounds of shuffling feet, whispered voices, and rustling robes surrounded her.

The scribes all but sputtered, beyond furious. The apprehension grew heavier, until finally, one stone dropped. The thud, as it landed on the tile, reverberated in her soul.

She opened her eyes just as Benaiah turned to go.

The Pharisee followed.

What was happening? Why would they leave?

The scribes looked from one to another, clearly not wanting to give up but not wanting to go forward without their leader.

Another stone dropped. One of the elder scribes glared at her before walking away.

It happened again and again, the oldest men first...until only Yana was left with the young rabbi.

When the footsteps faded, Yana sat up, clutching the cloak to her. None of her accusers remained.

They seemed to have been frustrated with the rabbi, though why was beyond her. They said he was teaching the law. How could that anger them?

Fist-sized rocks surrounded her in a messy half circle. She shuddered as she silently noted each one, imagining them hammering her body, breaking bones, and inflicting unbearable pain. She would not have survived even half of them.

The rabbi stood and extended a hand. She leaned on one palm, the other clasping her only garment, then pulled her feet underneath herself. He was being kind, but surely he wouldn't really want to touch a woman such as she, would he? Rabbis and scribes and all other leaders were always so obsessed with being ritually clean. She would bring far too much impurity to him.

She could just leave. Those who accused her had.

She could try to explain. Would it matter? She *was* guilty, no matter her reasons, no matter the behavior of the scribes.

She could stay and face the rabbi, face the consequences.

She should thank him. But how did she address him? "Rabbi" didn't seem enough. "Ba'al" wasn't right either. He was more than a master, more than just a teacher.

He spread his arms and looked around them. "Dear woman, where are they? Is there no one left to condemn you?"

She scanned the empty portico. "No one, lord."

The rabbi remained silent for several long moments.

Had he heard her? Did he expect something else?

He looked down on her with a smile that eased her fear. With gentle eyes, softer than Xander's. Kinder even than Ezi's.

Never had she been offered—or even seen—such mercy.

"Then neither do I condemn you. Go now and leave your life of sin." He reached to touch her shoulder then strolled toward the others.

That was it? Simply a gentle command to live a life without sin?

No stoning?

No public shaming?

Not even a lecture?

What kind of teacher was this man?

CHAPTER TWENTY

There is a way that appears to be right,
but in the end it leads to death.
~ Proverbs 14:12 ~

Head down, Yana trudged across the long walkway toward home. The upper city's residents headed for shops and the market. It was more crowded than her first journey across the bridge an hour ago, but at least this time she donned a cloak. Hopefully she'd be home before the entire city witnessed her disgrace.

But where she was headed was no longer her home. Never had been, really. There had not been one day she felt like she belonged there. It had always been Oded's home. He merely allowed her to live there.

But now where would she live? How would she care for Sarai?

She clutched at the borrowed garment and tried to quicken her steps as much as she could with bloody feet and bruised legs.

She stepped off the bridge, thankful for the narrow, uninhabited streets of the upper city. When she reached the street on which Oded's house sat, she turned left. All too soon, she stood in front of his wide, engraved double gate. Hoping to avoid talking to anyone, she pushed open the gate rather than knock.

Oded waited in his atrium. He never waited for anything. And why wasn't he in Ein Gedi? How did he know she was coming back at this very moment?

Then she saw him. Benaiah. He must have raced here as fast as his old legs would carry him once he fled the portico.

One of the scribes came out from Oded's workroom.

Another spy.

Oded's face reminded her of the hyena she'd once seen ready to pounce on a mouse. "Since you are alive, it appears I must give you this. A little more work for me, and for him"—he chuckled as he pointed to the scribe—"but the end result is the same." He handed her a rolled parchment, a red wax seal over a ribbon around the middle.

She broke the seal and opened it, though she couldn't read it.

"It's your certificate of divorce by reason of adultery." He leaned nearer and smirked. "I told you I would never give you back your dowry."

Her chest constricted like a giant hand was crushing her heart. "You *wanted* this to happen?" Did he ever go to Ein Gedi? Or had he stayed in Jerusalem, waiting for his plan to be put into action?

He didn't answer but continued smirking.

A sickening thought entered her mind. "Did you *ask* Xander to do this?"

He laughed loudly. "I didn't have to. I saw the way he looked at you, and I knew it wouldn't take much for him to bring you into his bed."

Her mind spun with questions, with denials. "But why? For two years I have done everything you've asked. I refrained from going to Bethany—until Simeon faced death. I wore your perfumes and your fine tunics and your jewels to temple to proclaim how very successful you are. I talked to no one but your family and did nothing but weave. I gave up the sun on my skin and the gurgling of the river and the wind through the trees and stayed hidden in your house." She felt physically ill. "I gave up nursing my own daughter."

He nodded. "Yes, you did. You did everything." He leaned over her. "Everything but give me a *son*."

Talking to him was accomplishing nothing. She didn't want to stay and she didn't want his money—her money. She wanted only to disappear.

Tugging the cloak around herself more tightly, she gathered all her resolve. "May I gather my things?"

"You will take only what you brought into this house. Which, I believe, was nothing."

That was fine with her. She desired nothing from this house. Something to wear on her way out was all she needed.

Naomi stepped forward. "There were several tunics you presented to her as a wedding gift, as I recall. Those are hers. As well as anything else you gave her as a gift."

Yana's head whipped around. For the second time, Naomi had defended her. Why?

"Very well. You may take them." He gestured to Naomi as he moved toward his workroom. "Imma will check your things before you leave to ensure you have not stolen anything."

She was afraid to ask her next question. "My daughter... Do you intend to keep her as well?"

He turned, scoffed. "You may have her. A daughter is of no use to me. Whatever you do, make it quick. I want you out of my house." He glared at her one last time before storming off.

Yana turned to Naomi. "Did you know?" It would explain why it was so easy to get time alone with Xander.

She raised her chin. "Not at first. I suspected he planned something when he said we would spend the night in Ein Gedi, but by the time I realized what he intended we were too far away. There was nothing I could do to stop it."

"But you approved?"

"I did not." Her eyes softened. "You may not have been the wife I would have chosen for my son. It may have taken longer than it should have, but I did everything I could to accept you, even to help you. If you knew how many times I talked to him about his treatment of you...but all he cares about is his business and how he appears to others." She shook her head. "Just like his own abba."

She walked several strides away and turned back to face Yana. "That does not mean, however, that I condone your behavior. No matter how badly he acted, your decision was wrong."

Yana's cheeks burned. Naomi was right.

Naomi shook her head. "But he could have handled it so differently. I truly am sorry for what happened to you. He should have just sent you away."

He should have treated her like a wife and not a stranger, a concubine. Still, she was wrong. She bowed her head. "I apologize for dishonoring you and your family. That was never my desire."

"I know."

"May I ask what happened to Xander?"

"Oded sent him to oversee the balsam groves in Ein Gedi."

"He didn't... Did he hurt him?"

Naomi shook her head. "No. Xander is too good at what he does for Oded to risk losing him."

Yana nodded. At least when it came to Xander, Oded's selfishness seemed to have paid off.

Basya waited for Yana at the bottom of the stairs. "Let me help you upstairs and get you cleaned up." She led Yana to the stairs, holding her elbow as they climbed. Yana's knees ached with every step.

In Yana's chamber, Basya remained silent as she retrieved a bowl of water and a cloth. She invited Yana to sit on the bed, then knelt facing her. She lifted one bloody foot and gently washed it. The water stung the abrasions covering the tops of her feet.

Yana hunched her shoulders and chewed her fingernails. She tried to avoid Basya's gaze as she cleaned the other foot. How could Basya be so kind after what she had done?

Basya rose up on her knees and reached for Yana's arm.

Yana's trembling intensified as Basya drew the damp cloth down her arms, removing blood, dirt, and grime. If only her shame could be washed away so easily.

By the time Basya reached for her other arm, Yana was shaking like a leaf in a spring windstorm. Basya set the cloth aside and pulled her close.

The tears Yana had been fighting for so long burst from behind closed eyes. Shame, regret, and guilt mixed with rejection, loneliness, and fear. Months—years of emotion poured from her like a river overrunning its banks. She gripped Basya's tunic and buried her head in her neck.

Basya held her until she calmed, rubbing her back, shushing her like a small child. When Yana pulled away, Basya offered a smile, wiping Yana's tears with her sleeve as she held her face. "I'm so sorry you felt you had to do this."

Yana believed her.

Basya threw a side-glance at the shut door. "Oded is a horrible person. Eventually something had to happen, as it did with his first wife."

The skin on Yana's neck prickled. His first wife. What didn't she know? "I thought he just divorced her."

Basya picked the cloth back up to wash Yana's face. "He did, but he had to return her dowry. He was livid. He spent weeks talking to Naomi's abba and brothers, trying to find out how he could make her responsible so he could keep the money. I guess this time he decided he didn't want to risk that. Yours was quite large, I understand."

Yana nodded. "Since most of it came from him in the first place."

"Let's get you dressed and packed. If we tarry much longer, his anger will be kindled again."

Yana stood and removed the cloak. "I don't want anything from here."

Basya held out a clean tunic. "You may as well take a few of the tunics. Who knows when—or if—you'll get any others?" She fingered the cloth. "Certainly none as nice as these."

Basya had a point. Still, she wanted nothing.

Yana pulled the simplest of the tunics over her head. No need to draw any more attention to herself by wearing bright yellow or deep red. She slid on the plain leather sandals she'd purchased and shrugged into her cloak.

"You pack what you want while I get Sarai ready for you." Basya slipped out the door.

Yana glanced around the room. There was really nothing she wanted. And he'd said she could have only the wedding gifts he gave her.

The only thing she wanted—other than her daughter— was the alabaster jar of perfume Ezi had given her as they said their final goodbyes. She wrapped it in another tunic and dropped it into the bag. If necessary, she could sell it for food. A bottle of expensive nard would be worth quite a bit.

Would she really sell it for food? Was it even wise to keep it because it reminded her of Ezi?

Not only Ezi but Bethany and everything in it. The life and land and people she loved.

She made her way downstairs to the nurse's chamber. The door was ajar, and Basya sat with the older woman. "I'm here for my daughter." Dalya slipped the babe into her arms. Sarai cooed, chubby arms reaching for Yana's face. Basya held out a small bag. "Her clothes. Some toys."

Dalya smiled. "You're a good mother. She'll be far better off with you than with her abba."

Yana blinked. "Th-thank you." Never once had Dalya offered a single word—or even a nod—of approval. "But this morning when I saw you, you scowled and turned away."

She stroked Sarai's hair. "I didn't want her to see you like that. And I was frowning at them and what the ba'al had done, not at you."

"Oh." Not that she didn't deserve Dalya's disapproval, at least for last night. "Thank you then, for keeping that from her. For caring for her these last months."

"You're welcome. Shalom, Eliyanah."

Yana stepped out of Oded's courtyard gate into the narrow streets. The gate latched shut behind her.

Now what?

Bewildered, she looked up and down the alley. She had no idea where to go. She had no home. No husband. No family. No money.

CHAPTER TWENTY-ONE

The wise woman builds her house,
but with her own hands the foolish one tears hers down.
~ Proverbs 14:1 ~

O nce again, Yana had acted without thinking through all
the consequences.

Ezi had warned her.

She'd ignored him, and she had lost everything.

She couldn't take her shame to Bethany, taint everyone
there with her sin. How would she explain to Miriam and
Marta that she had been unfaithful, even to someone as cruel
as Oded?

No. She had created this dreadful situation herself, and
now she must find a way out herself.

She wandered down the empty streets of the upper city until
she reached the lower market. Sarai cooed and babbled, obviously
enthralled by the sights and sounds so different from the quiet of
Oded's house. People rushed by, vendors shouted, beggars
grabbed at the cloaks of anyone who looked like they had money.

Everything Yana could ever need was available here, but
she had no way to purchase any of it. If she hadn't spent all this
week's money at the wool market...

If she only had a little time, time to think, a warm place to rest without worrying whether she and Sarai would be safe.

Ketziah. Could she possibly…?

A glimmer of hope flickering in her heart, she headed for Ketziah's shop south of the temple. Yana had bought wool from her nearly every time she visited Bethany, until Oded ordered her to stay home.

Yana found the narrow stall, but it was empty. It had been quite a while since Yana visited her, and anything could have happened. She refused to think about all the horrible reasons the old woman might not be there.

She moved to the shop next to Ketziah's. "I'm sorry. Do you know what happened to Ketziah? Is she no longer selling here?"

"I have much better yarn than she does, and I will beat any price she gave you." The man behind the table flashed a bright smile.

"I'm not here to buy anything. I just need to find her."

"My memory might be better if I sold something this early in the day." He snickered.

"I really don't—"

"Just a small sample."

"I haven't any money!" Yana hunched her shoulders as people on all sides stared at her. She hadn't meant to shout so loudly. "I just need to talk to her." She lowered her voice. "Please, can you tell me where she might be? Do you know where she lives?"

The man frowned. Was he trying to decide if she was telling the truth?

Finally, he pointed south. "She lives in the lower city, near the wall. That's all I can tell you."

When she reached the tiny houses beyond the southwestern corner of the temple, the poorest section of town, she went straight to the houses against the wall. There was nothing else to do except knock on some doors. She started down the row, asking everyone who answered where she could find the woman who sold yarn dyed the colors of sunset. Most simply grunted and slammed the door.

Maybe she should just give up. But what else could she do? Where would she go?

She knocked on yet another door. A young woman answered. "I'm looking for Ketziah, the woman who sells yarn in the wool market."

The woman furrowed her brow, staring at the babe in Yana's arms. "There are many Ketziahs in the city."

"I'm seeking the one who sells the brightly colored wool, who has a daughter and grandson." Sarai cooed and grabbed at Yana's cheek, and Yana stilled her hand.

The woman narrowed her eyes. "And why do you seek her?"

Yana felt her throat burning but swallowed the bile. "I need help," she whispered. "I didn't know where else to go."

The woman's face softened. "Ketziah is my mother. She's at the market now. Did you look there?"

The hope that had so briefly raised its head was crowded out by fear. "I just returned from there. No one had seen her yet today." What kind of message was she delivering? Was the woman hurt? Lost?

The woman smiled and waved a hand. "Then she went to buy more wool. With so many coming to the city for the feast, we sold almost everything we had yesterday. She'll probably bring it back here before she returns to the market so I can start dyeing it." She stepped back. "Would you like to come in?"

"Thank you." Yana stepped into a house that was even smaller than where she'd lived in Bethany. There appeared to be only one room. Half was open to the sky, which left half of a roof for use in the hot, dry season. How long had it been since Yana slept under the stars?

"I am called Adira. What kind of help do you need? May I help you?"

She didn't know this woman. What would her reaction be? "I'd rather wait for her, if I may."

"Of course. I'll get you something to eat." Adira moved to the corner. A shelf attached to the wall contained a few jars. A grinding quern and handstone sat on the floor beside a large cooking pot.

A small boy jumped down the ladder and raced through the room and to the street outside.

Adira chuckled as she brought Yana two pieces of flatbread and some goat cheese. "That was my son, Gavriel, who just burst out of here."

"How old is he?"

"This is his fourth year. My husband died before he was born." Adira smiled weakly. "He looks just like his abba, though. I thank Adonai for that every day."

Yana pulled Sarai closer. Would she ever look like Oded? Would Yana ever be thankful for that?

"Gavriel!" Outside, Ketziah called to her grandson. "Come here." Her laugh could be heard down the street.

She walked in with a bag over one shoulder and Gavriel in her arms. "Yana, motek! What are you doing here?"

The boy kissed Ketziah's cheek and squirmed down before going back outside.

Shame washed over her. "I'm in trouble. I need your help."

"Whatever I can do. You have helped me more than you know."

How? "What did I do?"

"Word spread that a rich woman from the upper city was buying my yarn. I have more buyers now than I can handle!" She cackled again, a familiar sound that brought joy in the midst of sorrow. "So what can we do for you?"

"I...um, my husband has divorced me. I have nothing and nowhere to go, and I was wondering if I could possibly sleep on your floor for a night or two until I figure out what to do. I know I'm asking a lot, but—"

"Nonsense. Of course you will stay here as long as you need."

Relief flooded her. At least she would be safe for a while.

She'd figure out what to do next in a few days.

Month of Chesvan
Mid Fall, AD 32
Jerusalem, Judea

In the last month, Yana had been welcomed into Ketziah's home as one of their family. She'd washed, carded, and even spun wool. She'd ground grain, made bread, and cooked barley stew—which surprisingly tasted pretty good—and in between nursed Sarai several times a day. The sun and the breeze kissed her skin, and women's laughter and children's giggles filled the air. She fell onto her reed mat each night exhausted, Sarai beside her, and drifted off to sleep, satisfied she'd accomplished something.

It was everything she'd missed in Oded's house. So why wasn't she more content?

She pulled off her cloak and hung it on a peg as she entered the house. "How was she?"

"Perfect, as always." Adira kissed the babe's cheek before she returned Sarai to her imma. "And how was my imma? You delivered the yarn?"

"Just in time. She'd sold nearly everything, especially the red-yellow kind."

"That's the favorite. Ever since you bought it, everyone loves it."

"Let me feed her, and then I can help you."

Scattered thoughts settled in her mind as she nursed her babe. Calm overtook her and for just a few moments, everything else faded.

Sarai slept beside her while Yana dunked raw wool into the soapy water and rubbed the fibers against each other to remove the lanolin. The greasy substance kept wool from becoming waterlogged and too heavy for the animal to bear, but that also meant the fibers would not hold dye and had to be removed.

Adira neared her and rubbed her fingers in several spots. "I think it's clean now. Rinse it well and then you can dye this batch I carded while you were at the market."

"Me?"

Adira smiled. "Sure. Wouldn't you like to learn?"

Yana had assumed their process to achieve such remarkable colors was a family secret, so she had never asked to be shown what they did, even though she'd washed what felt like camel-loads of wool in the last weeks. She dipped the wool in clean water until all the suds were gone, wrung it out, and spread it out to dry before joining Adira at the fire.

The woman's eyes brightened. "Show me what to do now."

"All right." Yana picked up the freshly washed wool and tried to remember the process she'd observed nearly every day since she'd arrived. "We need the same amount of dye as wool, so first I weigh it out." She placed the damp wool on one side of a balance scale, then added the chopped, dried madder root until the sides were equal.

"Yes. And next?"

"Boil the root first." She picked up the plate from the scale and poured the plant matter into the gently boiling water. An earthy, sweet scent Yana had come to love saturated the air. "When all the color has been boiled out, we remove the plant and add cool water first then the wool. Then...I'm not sure."

"Slowly bring it back to a boil then let it simmer until we get the color we want." Adira nodded. "I'll start washing another batch while you do that."

Yana rubbed her arms. Wet wool was deceptively heavy, and she'd been lifting and wringing it out all morning. Even though she'd been washing wool for Ketziah and Adira for a month, her arms still ached at the end of the day. The actual dyeing wouldn't be any less strenuous, but it was incredibly satisfying to see creamy wool become so beautifully colorful.

The madder relinquished all its color, and Yana fished out the plant pieces. Then she added a pitcher of cool water, and when the dye batch had cooled, she moved the uncolored yarn from the scale to the pot.

She dropped to the floor and tucked her legs under her next to a wide piece of leather the family used as a table.

Adira joined her and placed a platter of flatbread between them. "Yana, we love having you stay here. Do you know that?"

She slowly twisted to face Adira. Why would she ask? Was she going to send her away? She had, after all, intended to stay only a few nights. "Yes. Why?"

"I'm just wondering why you don't want to go home. You're welcome to stay here as long as you need to, and we would miss you very much if you left. But wouldn't you rather be with your family?"

Yana shrugged. "I have no family."

"You've never said one word about your life before you married. Where were you before you moved here?"

"Bethany."

"And you have no one there?"

Yana picked at the red madder stains on her fingers. "When I was a child, my abba moved us to Bethany from

Galilee. Shortly after, he left us. My imma remarried, to another Galilean, and then they returned there after my wedding."

"Surely there is someone who cared for you, who would want you to come back."

She thought about Simeon, about Miriam and Marta. They would take her back with open arms, but she wouldn't do that to them.

Sarai began to fuss. Yana picked her up and held her on her shoulder, gently rocking her.

Adira's son scooted closer and shook a clay rattle near her face.

"Gavriel, leave Sarai alone while she's trying to sleep. You can play with her after she sleeps a bit." Adira shooed him outside.

"Can I eat first?"

"Perhaps you should have eaten instead of playing with the baby."

Gavriel crossed his arms and compressed his lips into a pout.

Adira laughed. "Of course."

Yana gently patted Sarai's back until she settled once again.

Life here was good. She was loved, she was useful. She was safe and warm and fed.

It wasn't Bethany, but it was as good as she deserved.

CHAPTER TWENTY-TWO

The LORD's curse is on the house of the wicked,
but he blesses the home of the righteous.
~ Proverbs 3:33 ~

Yana placed a tiny piece of fig in Sarai's mouth as the babe sat in Gavriel's lap. Sarai frowned at the new texture, gummed it a moment, then smiled and cooed at the sweet taste.

Gavriel laughed as the baby flailed her arms for more.

Yana chuckled with him and pulled apart more pieces of the fig, setting them on a pottery plate. "Here, Gavriel, you can feed her." She gathered the rest of the meal's dishes and rose to go clean them.

"Imma, Yana, look!" Gavriel laughed and pointed to Sarai, her chubby cheeks smeared with purple pulp.

Adira handed a clean rag to Gavriel, who only succeeded in further spreading the sweet liquid.

Life had settled into a predictable and comfortable routine. Ketziah stayed at the shop, Adira continued dyeing wool, and Yana helped wherever necessary—at the shop, buying more wool, preparing meals.

Yana lit an oil lamp just as Ketziah entered. "Shalom, Ketziah. Good day?"

"Another excellent day. We're selling twice as much as usual with your help." Ketziah patted Yana's back.

"Well, you're giving me a place to live. It's the least I can do." Yana laughed.

Adira placed bread, cheese, and goat's milk on the mat. "Is the stew ready?"

Yana lifted the lid on the large pot balanced on rocks over a low fire. She stirred it once, releasing the scents of garlic, onions, and leeks. The lentils and barley were hot and soft, infused with flavor.

"I'm hungry!" Gavriel held his bowl in the air, his face a picture of anticipation.

"Prayers first, Gavi."

"Yes, Imma."

Gavi raised his chubby fists toward the sky.

"Blessed are You, Lord our God, King of the universe, who creates the fruit of the ground." Ketziah's gentle voice recited the age-old invocation. Though she spoke the same words multiple times a week, each time the prayer sounded as if it were newly crafted in her heart. "Blessed are You, Lord our God, King of the universe, through whose word everything comes into being."

"Now?"

Yana chuckled as she took the bowl from the boy. "Yes, motek, now."

The meal was nearly finished when a loud pounding on the door startled Sarai, and she began to cry. Adira went to the door.

Yana bounced Sarai on her knee and shushed her.

"I'm sorry, I don't think we can do that," said Adira.

"Please! You must help me." A young woman pleaded with Adira.

I know that voice.

"I have to see her." The woman at the door spoke again.

Diana.

Yana put Sarai in Gavi's lap and rushed to the door. "Diana! What are you doing here?"

"Yana!" Sobbing, Diana threw herself into Yana's arms.

"Come inside." Yana placed her arm around her shoulders and drew her inside, closing the door behind them. "How did you find me?"

"I just kept asking until someone told me where Ketziah lived. I hoped if I found her, she might be able to help me find you."

"What's wrong? Did something happen?"

"I just can't stay there anymore." Tears streamed down her face as she pulled up a sleeve to reveal a bruise on her forearm. "Without Xander to protect me... I'm so afraid of what he will do."

Diana didn't need to explain. Yana knew better than most.

"I had to leave, but I have no idea what to do now. I have some money, but it won't last forever."

"Let's just get through tonight. We'll discuss this more in the morning."

"Are you hungry?" Ketziah held up a plate of bread.

"Not really." Diana took one piece and sat beside Ketziah. She ripped off a piece, and within moments she had devoured it all. "I guess I was hungrier than I thought." She chuckled through tears.

"Eat all you want." Adira pushed the cheese and milk closer to Diana. "We know what you did for Yana. Thank you for helping her."

Diana shot Yana a quick glance, and Yana barely shook her head. She could trust Diana to keep her secret.

They knew Diana had helped Yana after Oded beat her, but they had no idea how great her own sin was.

Right now they could give Diana a place to sleep and some food for a few days.

But then what?

The tiny house was now even more crowded than usual, and Yana had lain awake most of the night. In the shadowy hours of dawn, she had reached a decision, and she wasn't at all sure it was the best choice. But she could think of nothing else.

Sarai squirmed beside her, and Yana rolled on her side and pulled her daughter close to suckle her.

Adira and Ketziah rose and poked at the fire, sending embers into the air and spreading what little heat it still carried. They set out yesterday's bread along with some goat cheese.

Sarai satisfied, Yana sat up and set Sarai beside her.

Gavi crawled closer. "Shalom, baby Sarai."

The babe giggled and reached for his face.

Sarai would miss her new playmate.

Yana chewed on a bite of cold bread. "Adira, Ketziah, I need to tell you something." She cleared her throat. "You've given me shelter, love, and food, and I can't begin to tell you what this has meant to me."

"But…?" asked Ketziah.

"I think I need to go back to Bethany."

"I thought you said you could never go back," Adira said.

"I did say that. But there are too many of us now. I think I should take Diana with me to Bethany." She ripped off another piece of bread and placed it on her tongue.

Diana grabbed her arm. "I'm not staying here. I'll leave today. Don't do this because of me."

"And where will you go?" asked Yana.

Diana shrugged. "I'll think of something."

Yana shook her head. "We both need a place to live. And I know we can live in the bet. That's what it's for."

"They won't let me stay there. I'm not even Jewish."

"Bethany has never turned anyone in need away." The words she had spoken to Rada at the bet two years ago echoed in her mind. *As long as there is Bethany, you will have a home.* "Besides, I think you're right, Adira. I need to be with family. I want Sarai to know her cousins. I want her to grow up as I did, working hard, helping others, laughing with family."

Ketziah nodded. "We'll miss you terribly, but I do think you're making the right decision."

"The only thing is…" Yana's voice wavered. "The last time I was home, Simeon—I told you about him—had gone to the caves."

Adira's hand went to her throat. "The caves? For those with tsara'at?"

Yana nodded. "I don't even know if he's still alive."

"Some of those people can live for years."

"I know. Others last only weeks. I haven't been back to Bethany since I first saw him there." The memory of him in rags, with unkempt hair but wearing a bright smile, haunted her. "I have to know." She shoved aside thoughts of the pain that could be waiting for her.

"We'll leave this afternoon."

Month of Chesvan
Mid Fall, AD 32
Bethany, Judea

At the top of the Mount of Olives, Yana looked back at Jerusalem. If she never saw that city again, she would be happy.

Diana sidled up next to her. "Regrets?"

"None. If none of it had happened, I wouldn't have her." She kissed a sleeping Sarai. "We're almost there."

They quickly reached the edge of the village.

She turned to scan the hillside to her left, across the road. From here she could make out the mouths of the various caves, gaping maws that sucked out the life of those already most miserable.

Yana inhaled a deep breath. She made sure the sling was securely around Sarai's little body. She didn't want to risk dropping her if emotion overtook her.

"Do you want me to hold her?"

Even better. She pulled the sling over her head and allowed Diana to take the baby. "Wait for me here." She put one foot in front of the other and paused. She summoned all her courage and kept walking toward the caves of Bethany.

The quiet unnerved her. Where were the calls of "Unclean! Unclean!" the law required? The plaintive voices should have begun their ritual moments ago.

Fear wrapped around Yana's heart, but she refused to entertain the worst possibility.

Slowing her walk, she neared the first cave. No one met her to warn her away. She peered through the dark, searching for a body, any body.

She saw no one.

Her heart began to pound, sending a slow, powerful pulse throughout her body.

She stepped away and searched the openings. Which one had Simeon occupied? She hadn't paid much attention then, as the others had directed her to him as soon as she drew even remotely near.

She closed her eyes, trying to remember anything she could bring to mind about the cave he'd come out of. *The rock.* There had been a large pointy rock to the right of the entrance. She searched frantically for it.

There.

She hurried down the line until she reached the rock that guarded Simeon's cave.

No one came to greet her.

"Simeon!" She tried to keep her voice from showing her panic. "Simeon!"

Where was he? Her heart sped up to twice its usual rate. Her thoughts churned. Even if Simeon... She couldn't bring herself to even think the words. But *all* of them?

She raced back to the village's lonely road.

"Yana!" Diana's voice called after her, but she didn't want to stop. The sun was nearing the horizon, and young boys stared as they led sheep to their homes to spend the chilly night in the warmth of the family home.

Simeon's courtyard was empty. She spun in a slow circle, searching for any sign of life. It would be too much to hope they were rescuing another donkey.

She retraced her steps back to the bet, Diana hurrying to keep up. Surely with Marta and Miriam visiting each day, the women here would have the latest news. She pushed open the gate and entered.

Empty. But the smell of fresh bread and warm lentil stew tickled her nose. An enormous pot sat on rocks over a low fire. Yana breathed a long sigh of relief. Sabbath preparations were underway.

Rada came from the house, a large wooden spoon in her fist. She headed toward the firepit, her eyes first catching Sarai in Diana's arms, then drifting to Yana's face. Recognition came slowly, then a smile burst across her face. "Yana!" She dropped the utensil and raced to embrace her.

"Rada, shalom."

Rada stepped back. "I'm so glad to see you. It's been so long."

"I'm happy to see you, especially up and cooking. But first, can you tell me where Si—" She choked on the name, unprepared for the painful answer Rada might have. "Miriam and Marta are?"

"They're at the temple. They go every week before Sabbath." She glanced at the sun. "They should be back soon, though. It's getting dark."

"Oh." She'd just have to wait.

"You can wait here." She drew the back of a finger down Sarai's cheek. "And who is this beautiful creature?"

Yana's fear was replaced by pride and love. "This is my daughter, Sarai. The one holding her is my friend, Diana."

"Shalom, Diana." Rada smiled. "She looks like you, Yana. May I hold her?"

"Of course." Diana transferred the squirming bundle.

"It's been a long time since mine were so little. My children have children, but..." Rada's voice was wistful. Sarai played with the lock of hair that had fallen from Rada's headcloth, and Rada laughed. "You should come home more often."

It had been a while since Yana thought of Bethany as home, but it still was more home than Jerusalem. "I may be around more from now on."

If all goes well.

"Wonderful! What do you think, Sarai? Do you want to stay here with us?" Rada tickled the baby's tummy and Sarai giggled.

She didn't ask why. The women of the bet learned not to ask too many questions. They just accepted each other's presence as a gift.

Noises from the road drew their attention, and Yana spun to face it.

"Go to them. Sarai and Diana can stay here while you catch up."

"Are you sure?"

"Of course. She's a delight. We'll bring her down in a bit."

"All right." Yana hurried down the path, pausing when she reached the main road to search the crowds for the familiar forms of Marta and Miriam.

She looked down the row of worshippers straggling into town. Many had already turned into their houses. She scanned those already past her and finally saw the sisters, arm in arm, heading toward the last house in town.

She raced to catch up. She wanted to call out but was reluctant to draw any attention to herself.

She grabbed Marta's shoulder. "Marta!"

Marta spun around, as did Miriam. The man next to them turned as well.

Simeon?

Yana felt all the air rush from her chest. Simeon was alive? He stood straight and tall before her, clothes clean, hair and beard trimmed, eyes bright with joy.

She dared not speak his name lest she awaken from a wondrous dream.

"Yana?" He stepped toward her.

"Uncle Simeon?" She stared at him through blurred eyes.

"Yes. It's me." He laughed.

Her knees buckled. It was a good thing she'd left Sarai with Rada, because she could hardly hold herself up. "What…? How…? But, but…" Bits and pieces of sentences spilled from her open mouth. None of this made any sense.

Miriam giggled. "I know how you feel." She frowned. "Where's Sarai?"

"She's… Umm… She's at…" She jerked her thumb over her shoulder.

"At the bet?"

Yana nodded.

Miriam touched her shoulder as she passed. "I'll get her."

Simeon wrapped his arm around her shoulders and led her toward his home. "Come, motek, and we'll tell you all about it."

CHAPTER TWENTY-THREE

He was despised and rejected by mankind,
a man of suffering, and familiar with pain.
Like one from whom people hide their faces
he was despised, and we held him in low esteem.
~ Isaiah 53:3 ~

"So he just *healed* you? What do you mean, he healed you?"
Simeon passed a giggling Sarai to Miriam. "The rabbi has been to our house many times over the last two years or so. Eleazar brought Him here for Pesach after you left. We knew that He was the rabbi Ezi had been following, but that was all we knew." He reached for some of Marta's flatbread and ripped off a piece.

He continued tearing pieces off, remaining quiet for so long Yana wanted to shake him to get him to continue his story.

"At first He was just like all those who come to Pesach and stay in Bethany. He and His disciples went into the Holy City during the day and returned for the night. Then I noticed how He prayed before they ate. It sounded like the traditional prayer we all say, but instead of 'Adonai, our God, King of the Universe,' he said, 'Abba.' I talked to Eleazar about it."

Simeon paused again. "This may sound ridiculous to you, but I believe it with all my heart and mind and soul and strength." He fixed his gaze on her. "I believe He is the Messiah, the Son of Adonai, sent to save us from our sins."

She scoffed. "That's impossible."

"Why?"

Why? So many reasons… "For one, isn't the Messiah supposed to overthrow the Romans and restore the kingdom to Israel?"

"One of David's psalms says, 'Adonai has established his throne in heaven, and his kingdom rules over all.' The kingdom David—and the rabbi—talk about is not a kingdom of this world."

Enough of that. Back to the important question. "But how—and when—did he heal you?"

"I first started feeling like something wasn't right during the last rainy season."

"I remember."

"As I said, He and His followers have been here many times, for every festival in Jerusalem, but they didn't come last Pesach. So—"

"Why not?" If he was such a good rabbi, why forgo coming to Jerusalem for the most important feast of the year?

"The Jewish leaders are not happy with Him. They have been searching for a reason to bring Him before the Sanhedrin."

Yana flinched at the mention of a trial before the judges. She'd barely escaped that. Memories of men holding stones they intended to throw at her unclothed body until she was dead were still much too fresh.

And secret.

"They've even said among themselves they want to kill Him for His heresy and violations of the law. It is for this reason He does not claim in public to be the Messiah."

"But He did come here for the Feast of Tabernacles," added Miriam.

"And He was saddened when I was not here. My son didn't even know I was sick, let alone that I had moved to the caves. So that night before the first day of Sukkot, He came to see me, with Eleazar and a few of His followers. He called for me to come to Him, then He placed His hand on my head, and said I was clean. He did the same to the others and said we had to go to the priests to be declared clean. We went the next morning, but of course we had to wait for a week to return to our homes."

"And where are the others?"

"Most were from Jerusalem, and they went home to their families, happy and whole. Only one stayed here in Bethany. He has cousins here."

She shook her head. It was simply too much to believe.

Simeon's words defied every law of nature, everything she had ever learned or experienced.

The caves of Bethany emptied? Every man and woman healed in an instant? It just wasn't possible.

Yet there Simeon sat, as clean and perfect as a newborn baby. He looked even better than before he sickened. The joy he'd evidenced in the cave was doubled, at least, if that were possible.

"I would go through it all again—the pain, isolation, the suffering—just to experience the healing touch of the Messiah."

How could a mere man be the Son of God?

Yet the way they talked about him, he was far from a mere man. Healings, calmed seas, water to wine, thousands fed from a few loaves of bread and a couple of dried fish. Many of the stories Ezi had related to them on his visits to Bethany.

Miriam selected a dried fig and began peeling it.

"Yana, we haven't seen you here in so long. I thought your husband had forbidden you to come back here."

All her shame flooded back over her. How did she tell these people, the ones closest to her, who had showered her with love since the day she'd moved here, who she was now? *What* she was now?

She cleared her throat. "I no longer have a husband."

Miriam's hands stilled. An uncomfortable silence fell around them like heavy dew covering the first spring flowers.

"He divorced me the last day of the Feast of Tabernacles." The same week Simeon had been healed.

Miriam grabbed her hand. "Yana, I'm so sorry. What a horrible man."

"He hurt me.... When I received Marta's message about Simeon, he wouldn't let me come. I begged, I pleaded, but he would not relent. His imma told me to come, said she would convince him it was all right. But he came home while she was gone, and he beat me." She wasn't ready to recount the story about the priests, the scribes, and the young rabbi in the court again, let alone her unfaithfulness.

"So if that was during Sukkot, where have you been since?"

"I stayed with a woman and her daughter in the lower city. They were always very kind to me. She's a yarn merchant." She reached into the bag she'd brought. "They slipped some of her yarn into my bag. I've only seen such vibrant colors in her shop."

Yana withdrew the bright crimson and purple and yellow-red balls of woolen yarn. Perhaps this would change the subject for a while.

The girls oohed and ahhed over the yarn for a bit, but the subject soon returned to the man who healed lepers, calmed seas, and gave sight to the blind.

If she believed their stories.

But how could she not, sitting in Simeon's home and eating with him?

"So this rabbi... What else do you know about him?" They had better know a lot more before they started telling people he was the Messiah.

"He is from Nazareth. He's a builder by trade, but He has several wealthy followers—many women—who support Him as He teaches."

"Women disciples?"

"Yes! Isn't it wonderful?" Miriam's voice squeaked with excitement.

"A builder from Nazareth. That's all?"

"He has several brothers and a sister. His abba died long ago, but His imma still lives in Nazareth with His brothers."

"He doesn't sound all that different from any other rabbi who travels and teaches. Except for the women, maybe. That alone would be enough to make the priests hate him."

"No, no!" Simeon's face lit up. "He's completely different. Yeshua says—"

Yana grabbed Miriam's arm. "Yeshua?"

"Yes. Why?"

Her blood ran cold. "Son of...?"

"Yeshua ben Yosef."

No, please, Adonai, no. This could not be the same man.

Was this the same Yeshua Oded had talked about over two years ago? The one who had toppled the tables of the money changers and driven the animals from the temple courts?

Their perfect rabbi, who spoke of love and mercy, who healed the sick, was the same young rabbi who had dared confront the Pharisees and save her from a stoning. He was also the same Yeshua who had declared he would rebuild the temple in three days and whom the priests wanted to kill.

How could all these images of one man be reconciled?

The only way was to discount some of the stories Simeon and the girls had told her. They simply couldn't be true. Yeshua had to be a rabbi like any other, except that he appeared to enjoy antagonizing the Pharisees.

But what about Simeon? She'd seen him in the caves, and she saw him now.

He had been healed. Of that there was no doubt. How could she explain that?

How could anyone explain it?

Night was drawing near, and Yana had not mentioned her plans.

"We need to get going. Sarai is already asleep and we are tired as well."

Miriam frowned. "Going where? It's too dark for you to go anywhere, and besides, it's the Sabbath now."

"Diana, Sarai, and I will be staying at the bet."

Marta rose. "Don't be ridiculous. You're family. You'll stay here."

She shook her head. "No, I can't do that."

"Why not?" asked Simeon.

"I don't want my sin to stain you. You're the leader of the village. You can't have a divorced woman living in your home."

"And I am a leper who was healed."

"That was not your choice. It's different." She spread her hands. "We'll stay at the bet with the other women who have no choice. We can help with the food and their care."

Marta stepped nearer. "You can do that from here. Because you *do* have choices."

How could she argue her point without telling them everything? Without bringing even more shame upon herself and so also to them?

"You could stay in your old house. No one lives there," said Miriam.

"But I saw someone there."

Simeon nodded. "You might have. People have stayed there a few nights or so, but no one has lived there since Lemuel and your imma left."

Miriam grabbed her hand. "Come, I'll help you."

"I'll bring some blankets and some other things you might need. The house is almost completely empty." Marta hurried to the back of the house to gather the promised items.

Diana carried Sarai as the three women crossed the courtyard.

Yana held the bags she'd taken from Oded's in her fist, one of Sarai's things and a smaller one for herself. She set them on a sleeping bench, and a quiet clunk caught her attention. She pulled the white jar from the bag.

"I want to give this back to you." She offered Miriam the perfumed oil.

"What is it?" Miriam took it and held it up, examining it.

"It's a jar of nard." She paused. "Ezi gave it to me the day we said goodbye. I told him he should keep it, but he wouldn't take it back. Maybe you can convince him to take it."

"It's beautiful."

"Very expensive too, he said."

"I'll see what I can do." She smiled. "I can usually talk him into anything."

After Marta delivered the blankets, Yana lay on the bench, Sarai curled up to her chest.

She had no idea what would happen next, but she felt like she was home for the first time in two years.

Month of Kislev
Late Fall, AD 32
Bethany, Judea

A month in Bethany had soothed Yana's soul like a fragrant balm. She and Diana had moved into Yana's old house. Apparently whoever it was she'd met that day was only visiting. Marta and Miriam, as well as Diana, helped her with Sarai, who had learned to crawl and even walk, as long as someone held her hands and kept her upright.

The excited talk of Yeshua continued. Yana generally remained silent. The only point of contention was her stubborn refusal to go to temple each week before Shabbat.

"Are you sure you won't come with us?" Simeon tried to get her to give him a reason, but as with every time it came up, guilt and fear so overwhelmed her that her ears burned and she simply walked away.

She couldn't bring herself to relive the nightmare of that morning. "I think Sarai is still too young. She might cry and disrupt the evening sacrifice." That was not a good reason, but it was the only one she had. "We'll get the bread made for tomorrow. You go."

"Next week then? For the festival?"

"Of course."

It was clear, at least to Yana, that he didn't believe her, but he didn't push her. He and the girls left her and Diana at home and departed for temple.

Yana grabbed the extra flour they had ground this morning and headed for the courtyard oven.

"Why don't you go with them?" Diana followed, bent and holding Sarai's hands as the child toddled behind her imma.

"I'm sure you can guess why."

"And why does he want you to come next week? What festival is he talking about?"

Yana added more water and continued kneading the dough. "The Festival of Dedication is a commemoration of the Jews' revolt against the Syrian king. He decreed we must follow Syrian law and ordered pigs to be sacrificed on the altar, an unforgivable defilement of our temple."

"That's horrible!"

"Mattityahu, a priest, and his five sons led the revolt and recaptured the temple. His son Judah ordered the temple to be cleansed and a new altar built, after which the temple was to be rededicated to the Lord. Unfortunately just one flask of holy, undefiled oil was found—only enough oil to burn for one day. It would take eight days to prepare a new supply. Miraculously, when the priests poured in the oil and lit the menorah, it burned for eight days."

Because this feast was celebrated in homes, not the temple, Yana would have one more reprieve until Pesach. Sarai would be over a year old then, so she couldn't be Yana's excuse. But she had several months to come up with a reason not to go.

Yana ripped off a piece of warm bread and placed it in Sarai's hand. She'd been fussy for days, with a new tooth erupting through her tender gums. Warm bread was the only thing that seemed to help.

"I'll take her inside and see if she will sleep a bit before the meal."

"Thank you."

Diana walked Sarai to Yana for a kiss, then picked her up and headed for the house.

Yana continued cooking loaf after loaf of bread.

"She looks like you."

The voice behind her sent a chill down her spine. She froze, unable to move.

Could it be? She slowly turned to look over her shoulder.

Ezi.

What was he doing home? As soon as the question formed, she knew the answer. He—and Yeshua and all his disciples—would be here for the eight days of the festival.

She could only hope they would spend all their time—except while asleep—in Jerusalem.

"Shalom, Ezi."

His face brightened and a slow smile appeared. "Shalom, Yana."

She looked past him. "Where are the others?"

"The others?"

"Your rabbi and his followers."

"I usually come early so Marta is prepared to feed us all. Sometimes I go into the city for her to purchase supplies." He searched the courtyard. "Where's Abba? And my sisters?"

"They left for temple. You can catch them if you hurry."

"I will. Want to join me?" He jerked a thumb toward Jerusalem.

Not really. "I think I'll stay here with Sarai."

"I'll be back soon then. I can't wait to talk to you and hear about your life in Jerusalem." He hurried off.

So far, she'd managed to avoid talking about the incident in the temple.

But Ezi knew her better than anyone. He could always tell if she was lying, or even leaving something out.

Now she would have to figure out a way to tell him she had been unfaithful, dragged to the temple, and shamed before all of Jerusalem.

CHAPTER TWENTY-FOUR

As Jesus and his disciples were on their way,
he came to a village where a woman named
Martha opened her home to him.
~ Luke 10:38 ~

Yana strolled beside Ezi down Bethany's street, which was about as far as they could walk on the Sabbath.

From the way the muscle of his jaw twitched, he obviously had something to say but was worried about it.

"Just say it, Ezi."

"What?"

"You want to say something or ask something, but you don't want to hurt my feelings. Just say it."

He pursed his lips. "Miriam says you…are no longer married."

"True."

"Can I ask what happened?"

From the moment she'd heard his voice, she'd known there would be no way to avoid this conversation. Might as well get it over with. "Oded divorced me."

He nodded slowly. "Do you want to tell me what happened?"

She neared the well in the center of town. This time of day there should be no one coming for water, so she sat on the wide stone edge of the ancient watering place. "I was unfaithful." She picked at her nails, unable to look at him.

He had to be shocked, but he didn't let it show. "Yana, that's not like you. Why would you do such a thing?"

"It *is* like me. You're the one who said I made rash decisions, without thinking through the consequences." She hadn't meant for her voice to be so sharp.

He sat next to her, about an arm's length away. "Then why did you make such a decision?" His voice was gentle, not condemning. More like concerned, caring even. Like he was when he still loved her.

She twisted to face him and then told him about Oded. His inattention, the reason he married her, his ridiculous demands. "He never loved me." She shrugged.

"Could he have grown to love you?"

She quashed the anger rising in her chest. "I did everything I could to make it work. I tried to learn about his business. I did all that he asked. He said himself the only thing I didn't do was give him a son."

"But, Yana, many women in Israel have marriages that are not perfect."

She resisted jumping up and throwing her arms in the air. "Not perfect?" She glanced around the town center, regretting she had raised her voice. "This was so much more than not perfect. I am not defending my action, but, Ezi...he hit me. More than once." She ran her tongue over the scar on her lip.

His eyes dropped to her mouth, and he frowned. "I'm sorry."

"The last time was when I came home to see Uncle Simeon, when I received word he went to the caves. Oded forbade me, but I came anyway. Another bad decision, I suppose, but one I don't regret."

A light smile crossed his lips.

"Anyway, when I came back…I ended up with a black eye, bruised face, sore ribs."

"So that's when he divorced you?"

"No. I had asked him to divorce me, but he refused." She put her thumb to her mouth, chewing on the nail. "I haven't told anyone else this, not even Simeon."

"Yana, you don't have to tell me anything."

She wanted him to know, needed him to know. To understand.

"His servant Xander was so kind. I just craved a little kindness." She sniffled. "Oded knew Xander liked me. So he took everyone to Ein Gedi for the last night of Sukkot. The next morning…" Her voice broke. "A priest, with four scribes, burst into Xander's room and caught us. They punched Xander several times, and I was dragged, without my clothes, to the temple. Oded's sabba, Benaiah ben Shammai, met us at the temple. They intended to take me to the Sanhedrin to be tried, but they saw this rabbi teaching in Solomon's Portico and took me to him instead. I still don't understand why."

Ezi's eyes grew wide and his face paled. "That was *you*?"

Realization slammed her like a rock. "You were there?" How would she ever face him again? Maybe she should just jump into the well. "You saw me?"

"Not really. I was in the back of the crowd, and as soon as they brought you forward, we backed away. We didn't want to cause her—you—more embarrassment."

"And that was your Yeshua, the one you follow, that Simeon and the girls have been telling us about?"

She remembered the story of her first Pesach in Jerusalem. "He's the one who turned over the tables of the money changers?"

Ezi nodded.

"I don't understand. How can he be so violent with the money changers, who were not disobeying any laws, but let one who is obviously guilty go free with no punishment?"

"First, he wasn't violent. I was there. He was calm and quiet. He simply opened the gates to let the animals out. He made a short whip to drive the animals from the temple grounds, not the men. He did tip over the tables, because they don't belong on the grounds. They steal space reserved for the Gentiles. The vendors cheat people and demand a higher price than necessary. The temple is a place of worship, not a market, especially not a dishonest one."

"Oded told us he said the temple was his abba's house."

"He did. It is. He is the promised Messiah. I know that like I know the sun will rise tomorrow."

Ezi had never yet lied to her. But could his friend really be the Messiah?

"Even if I believe that, and I'm not sure I do yet, that doesn't explain why he simply told me to leave my life of sin and then let me go."

"He was trying to show them the extent of their hypocrisy. What they did was beyond evil. It was completely against the Law of Moses."

These men studied the laws, taught the laws. How could anything they do be illegal? "Why? I was guilty, regardless of why I did it."

"Yes, but there are rules. First, there must be at least two witnesses."

"There were. The priest brought along four scribes."

Ezi twisted to face her and his hands became animated, as they always had when he was excited. "All right, but then, it is these individuals who must be the first to put the accused to death. They must be willing to themselves deliver the punishment they request."

"Those who saw me?" The humiliation of that morning washed over her anew.

"Yes. Yeshua was telling them if they wanted to invoke the Law of Moses, as they said, they would need to *fully* follow the law, not just the parts they liked."

"Which means?"

"The witnesses must come forward and identify themselves. Their testimony is examined in detail to ensure it is the truth."

"It would have been."

"Yes, but they also become subject to all laws pertaining to false witnesses. If they do not tell the *whole* truth—that you were set up to be caught, that they were told when and where to find you by your husband—that is the same as lying, and they would then be subject to the same punishment as you— death by stoning."

She could see that, but that still didn't explain everything. "But I was still guilty."

"Yes, but their guilt was greater. Your sin was a result of weakness. You didn't set out to trick someone into sin and then lie about it."

Now it made sense. The oldest first realizing what they had done. The dropped rocks. The grumbles under their breath. The rushed footsteps leading away from her.

Ezi scooted closer and took her hands in his. "Yana, you are forgiven. All you have to do is believe that. And then, as He said, sin no more."

She blinked back tears and shook her head. "I can't be forgiven. My sin is too great."

"You know Abba's favorite saying of the prophets?"

"The one about singing?"

"Yes. Zephaniah says Adonai will quiet you with His love, He will rejoice over you. That means He will no longer rebuke you. He will calm your soul. King David said in one of his psalms, 'He has removed our sins as far from us as the east is from the west.' Adonai has forgotten your sins. Why can't you?"

Such a simple question. One she had no answer for.

Ezi squeezed her hands. "And you must tell your family what happened."

Yana shook her head. "No. I can't do that. Everyone will hate me." How could he even suggest such a thing?

"No one will hate you. I understand. They will too." Ezi grinned. "We love you, Yana. You're family."

"How can anyone understand what I did? Let alone *forgive* what I did?"

"I can. Yeshua did."

Why did everything always come back to Yeshua?

"Would you rather they hear it from you or as gossip?"

He had a point.

They headed back to the house, and Ezi led her inside. He gathered everyone and asked them to sit down.

"I have to tell you all something." She crossed her arms and chewed on her thumbnail. "I... The reason Oded divorced me is because I was unfaithful to him."

A couple of mouths dropped open, but no one said anything. There were no gasps, no shouts of condemnation.

Ezi leaned near. "Tell them everything, Yana."

Yana told them about Oded, Xander, and everything else the recent years had brought.

"Did you know he made her go to the temple alone for her purification after Sarai was born?" asked Diana.

"Yana, I'm so sorry." Miriam rose to embrace her, but Ezi stopped her.

"That's not all. Tell them about Yeshua and the temple."

"Yeshua? What does He have to do with this?" asked Simeon.

"Oded..." Her voice broke, and she angrily wiped away tears as she told them about the incident at the temple.

Simeon rose. "I am so sorry, Yana. That was not done according to law, in any way. It was wrong from beginning to end."

"That's what I told her," said Ezi.

Why didn't they understand? "But I was *guilty*. Their actions don't change that."

Simeon placed his hands on her shoulders. "No, they don't. But are you sorry for your actions?"

"Of course." What a foolish question.

"Then you are forgiven. All you need to do is as Yeshua said. As far as is possible, live your life without sin. You don't need to keep punishing yourself."

She shrugged. "I don't know."

"Motek, Adonai rejoices over you. Your very existence brings Him pleasure. Rest in that."

Simeon had been saying that for years, but she found it even harder now to believe than she did the first time. How could she ever bring Him any pleasure at all?

Marta rose. "I think we all need to get some rest. Yeshua and His disciples will be here the day after tomorrow."

Yana suppressed a groan. Could this day get any worse?

She'd stood naked before him, and though he hadn't shamed her, he certainly couldn't be pleased with her, no matter what Simeon—or Zephaniah—said.

And which Yeshua would he be? The one who threw tables, or the one who pardoned an unfaithful woman and touched the untouchable?

Either way, she wasn't at all sure she wanted to meet him.

CHAPTER TWENTY-FIVE

Then came the Festival of Dedication at Jerusalem. It was winter, and
Jesus was in the temple courts walking in Solomon's Colonnade.
~ John 10:22–23 ~

Yana felt very much as she did when she'd awakened on the roof of her house nearly three years ago. The day she dreaded was here. This time it was not the day of her wedding but the arrival of the man Simeon and Ezi said was the promised Messiah.

She felt ill.

Maybe she could just tell them she was sick and stay on the roof all day. But that would only get her out of today. No one would believe she was ill for eight days.

The sun was barely up, but there was much to be done. She sat up, pulled Sarai into her lap and suckled her, then wrapped her in her sling before going downstairs. Yana would be especially busy today, and Sarai would need to stay close.

The best thing to do was to keep working. They would need bread today, lots of it. They had many more people to feed—at least thirteen more, not to mention the bet. Ezi said Yeshua only brought his closest twelve with him when he left Galilee.

Yana poured barley into the hole in the grindstone, then set the donkey in motion. She filled bowl after bowl with flour before Miriam joined her and began mixing dough.

The familiar activities took her mind off of the visitors. For a while.

"When do you think they'll arrive?" asked Yana.

"If this time is like all the others, around midday."

Yana snuck a look at the sun. By the time they finished at the bet, the sun would be at its highest.

And she would have to face him.

The noise could only mean one thing. They had arrived.

Yana rubbed her fingers against her temples, trying to calm the raging pain in her head.

A large group of men entered the village from the south, the road that led to Jericho and Galilee. She ducked inside as they walked straight toward Simeon's house. Simeon, Ezi, and the girls all poured out of the house to greet them. Obviously, they'd been here many times. The love among all of them was evident.

Another low table had been set up in the courtyard, with cushions on all sides. Yeshua and his friends gathered around it, and Simeon and Ezi joined them.

Marta rushed past her. "Yana, will you help me carry the food out to them? They'll be ravenous after walking for four and a half days. I want to feed them before we go to temple."

Temple? "For the Feast of Dedication? We won't celebrate here?"

"We'll light the candles when we get back but we'll go to temple for the evening sacrifice first, as we do every week." She picked up a large basket of bread and headed outside.

Yana grabbed two wide, shallow bowls of olive oil. The men laughed and talked among themselves. Maybe he wouldn't notice her. All she needed to do was set the bowls down and leave. She crept toward the one end of the table and leaned over, leaving the oil.

The rabbi smiled up at her. "Thank you, Eliyanah."

She froze. She could ignore him. Pretend she didn't hear him.

No, she couldn't.

"Thank you." Her voice came out in a squeak.

"Your daughter is beautiful."

"Thank you." Now what? "I have to go feed her." She backed away and bumped into Marta with a platter of cheese.

"Yana? Aren't you going to eat with Miriam and Diana and me?"

"I-I'm not hungry. I'll go to my house where it's quieter and try to get her to sleep a while."

"All right. See you in a bit. You're coming with us, yes?"

She nodded and hurried away. The entire table had heard the conversation. All of them would be expecting her to go with them. How would she get out of this now?

Yana swallowed a sigh. Diana had offered to stay with Sarai, so she had run out of excuses. Though she'd hoped never to make this journey again, she trudged along the familiar road to the Holy City. Miriam walked beside her, and she clutched her arm.

Too soon, they reached the southern gate. They made the short trek up the stepped street and then climbed the long, wide stairway at the southwest corner of the temple that led to the Court of the Gentiles.

Yana's entire body tensed as she entered the court. She tried to forget about the last time, but the memories kept breaking through. Forcing herself to put one foot in front of the other, she finally reached the women's court.

Men and women worshipped in this court, as the Court of Israel was quite small. Only men offering sacrifices were allowed into the chamber that held the altar. In larger assemblies as this one, the women stayed toward the back and the men moved to the front.

Miriam slipped her arm through Yana's and led her toward the bronze doors of the Nicanor Gate. Simeon and Ezi passed her on their way to the front. The rest of the disciples followed.

Yeshua stopped beside her and leaned near. "Quiet your heart and you will hear Him singing over you." Then he moved on.

Her heart fluttered. How could he know that's what Simeon had told her?

The Levite choir filed in, filling the fifteen steps that led from the court to the gate. When all had assembled, they began singing the Hallel.

She looked toward the men. Yeshua stood with arms outstretched, face toward heaven, his voice strong and joyful.

From sunrise until sunset
Adonai's name is to be praised.
Adonai is high above all nations,
his glory above the heavens.
Who is like Adonai our God
seated in the heights,
humbling himself to look
on heaven and earth.

The rabbi knew the priests hated him, were plotting against him, but here he was praising Adonai.

Praising his *abba*, if she believed Simeon and Ezi.

Adonai is merciful and righteous;
yes, our God is compassionate.
Adonai preserves the thoughtless;
when I was brought low, he saved me.
My soul, return to your rest!
For Adonai has been generous toward you.

Adonai had been generous to her, and she hadn't even noticed. She was too busy feeling sorry for herself, moaning over what she had lost.

Yes, you have rescued me from death,
my eyes from tears and my feet from falling.
I will go on walking in the presence of Adonai
in the lands of the living.

I will keep on trusting even when I say,
"I am utterly miserable,"
even when, in my panic, I declare,
"Everything human is deceptive."

How did she begin trusting Him again when everything around her was deceptive? Even her own thoughts had deceived her.

She touched her head to the tile, her hands flat next to her head, listening to the holy psalms.

Yah is my strength and my song,
and he has become my salvation.
He has become my song.

The words Simeon had told her so long ago swirled in her head.

"He will take great delight in you; in his love he will no longer rebuke you, but will rejoice over you with singing."

How could He delight in her? No longer rebuke her? There was nothing she could do to make up for what she had done. She was a fallen woman, cast aside. Worthless.

The Levites were nearing the end of the Hallel. They would return to the beginning and keep singing until the sun fully set.

"Give thanks to Adonai, for he is good; for his grace endures forever."

Could His grace really outweigh her sin? Was His love that powerful?

My love for you is everlasting.

Wait. That was not the sound of the Levite choir.

My lovingkindness extends to the heavens, my faithfulness reaches to the skies.

The song was incomparably beautiful. But who was singing?

I am forgiving and good, abounding in love to all who call to Me.

She sat up. Adonai? Was this the voice of Adonai, singing over her?

Was she finally hearing it?

As an abba has compassion on his children, so I have compassion on those who fear me.

Had He always been singing? Had she just never been quiet enough to hear it?

She laughed as Adonai's words continued to flow over her, surround her, soak into her heart as dye became part of the wool.

He'd shown her mercy she didn't deserve. He had compassion for her. She was forgiven. A new life was hers.

My love for you is everlasting.

Boundless, never-ending love. Could anything be more wonderful?

Yana could have run up the Mount of Olives and down to get back to Bethany.

Her heart was full of song, overflowing with joy. Love saturated her soul. All she wanted was to get back to Sarai, to hold her, to love her as she herself was loved. Yana would teach her daughter as she grew how completely, irrevocably, unfailingly Adonai loved her. She would ensure Sarai knew it like she knew her own name.

And Diana. She needed to know too.

Eliyanah had wasted so much time by not listening to Him, for Him. Adonai's music was now so obvious, inescapable, so recognizable—how had she not heard Him before?

But He hadn't given up on her. He'd continued to call to her until she quieted enough to hear Him, and now the song was a part of her, as close as her heartbeat, her next breath.

The future was changeable, unreliable, but Adonai was not. And at last, Eliyanah could rest in His everlasting love.

AUTHOR'S NOTE

Can we ever make so many mistakes, so many bad choices, that God just gives up on us?

Of course not. We know that. But we often don't act like we believe it.

We don't know the name of the woman in John 8, but Jesus did. She was more than a label to Him, more than her sin. She was a child of God, created in His image. Jesus knew her every thought, all her pain, each fear, and He loved her more than we can possibly imagine.

He didn't condemn her. I believe she struggled with that. How long did it take her to truly, deeply believe God loved her and had forgiven her?

My husband has a saying he often repeats to our children.

"There are things you could do that would disappoint me, but there is nothing you can do that will ever make me not love you."

Our heavenly Father feels the same way. God's love is perfect, unfailing, never-ending, and He longs to lavish it on us, to rejoice over us in song.

We only need to be quiet enough to hear it.

—Carole Towriss

FACTS BEHIND the Fiction

❖

ESSENES, THE MONKLIKE JEWS

According to Josephus, a first-century Jewish historian, Essenes weren't into pleasure, wealth, or "the wanton ways of women," as Josephus put it. He said Essenes generally had low regard for women, "persuaded that none of them preserves her faithfulness to one man" [Jewish War, Book II, c. 8.2]. Nonetheless, a few did marry. Instead of getting married and having children, Josephus reported, some Essenes opted to adopt children of outsiders.

Essenes themselves were outsiders. They lived a lifestyle a bit like that of ascetic monks. Essenes deprived themselves of even basic comforts, such as olive oil skin moisturizer, which was commonly used in that dry part of the world. "They consider olive oil a stain," Josephus said. "Should anyone be accidentally smeared with it, he scrubs his body, for they make it a point of honor to remain hard and dry, and to wear white always."

QUMRAN SCRIBES COPYING
REPLACEMENT EDITIONS
OF WORN-OUT SCROLLS OF
SACRED JEWISH LITERATURE.

Like Pharisees and Sadducees, Essenes made up a separate sect of the Jews, embracing distinct teachings. They taught that God is responsible for everything that happens. And, unlike Sadducees, and like Pharisees, they said the soul lives forever.

About one hundred years before Christ, Essenes withdrew from the broad Jewish community that worshipped at the Jerusalem temple. They left after the leader of a Jewish political party—the Hasmoneans—declared himself high priest. Jewish law reserved that office for descendants of Aaron, Moses's older brother. So Essenes said Israel no longer had a legitimate religious leader.

Essenes settled in cities throughout the Jewish homeland, Josephus wrote. Many scholars say one group of Essenes founded Qumran, a small community near the Dead Sea. There, they prayed, studied, and made new copies of sacred but worn-out Jewish writings—including the now famous Dead Sea Scrolls. Among those scrolls, scholars discovered a copy of the book of Isaiah 1,000 years older than the version scholars had used to translate the King James

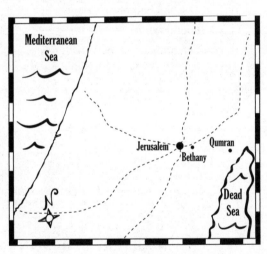

THREE OF THE LOCATIONS IMPORTANT TO ELIYANAH'S STORY

Version of the Bible. There were only minor differences in those two versions of Isaiah.

Essenes were tight-knit groups of people who pooled their local resources, as people do in a commune. Josephus said Essenes didn't experience "the humiliation of poverty nor the superiority of wealth... the assets of each one have been mixed in together, as if they were brothers, to create one fund for all."

DOUBLE STANDARDS IN ADULTERY

ADULTERY IN ROMAN TIMES: WOMEN

Roman and Jewish men wrote stern laws to protect themselves from wives who might pollute the family tree with someone else's child. Men didn't want illegitimate heirs inheriting their life's work. They didn't like the idea of someone trespassing on their property, which is what wives were in this patriarchal age.

A wife caught sleeping with anyone but her husband paid the price, which varied, from Roman to Jewish laws. The Roman emperor Augustus ordered all adulterous women tried in court. If found guilty, they were divorced and exiled to an island. But that law came back to bite Augustus when he had to exile his own daughter under this ruling.

A Roman father, by one law, could kill his adulterous daughter and the person she had slept with. The wronged husband could kill only the other man, and then only if that man came from a lower class in Roman society. It wasn't permitted for a plebeian commoner to execute a ruling-class patrician.

Jewish law, by comparison, ordered both sexual partners stoned to death. That wasn't usually tolerated under Roman rule, during Rome's occupation of what is now Israel and the Occupied Palestinian Territories. Jews were supposed to get the Roman governor's permission to execute someone.

ADULTERY IN ROMAN TIMES: MEN

Men suffered consequences for committing adultery. But Romans and Jews alike defined adultery for men as having sex with another man's wife. Unmarried women and prostitutes didn't count. On the other hand, Roman and Jewish men agreed that a woman committed adultery if she had sex with anyone other than her husband, married or not.

Men who engaged in adulterous acts were seen as trespassing on someone else's property—the wife—and that behavior could get a Roman man divorced and exiled, or a Jewish man divorced and executed.

JESUS WITH THE WOMAN
CAUGHT IN ADULTERY.

TEST OF THE BITTER WATER

If a Jewish woman suspected her husband of adultery and couldn't prove it, she couldn't do much about it beyond serving him bad food and a chilly bed. Women had to wait another 1,800 years for the first private detective agencies.

But a suspicious husband, on nothing more than a gut feeling, could march his wife straight to the Jerusalem temple for the test of the bitter water.

The priest would pour holy water into a clay jar and toss in some dirt from the temple floor. Then he wrote onto a scroll a curse, the punishment the woman would face if guilty: she wouldn't be able to have children. He scraped the ink of this curse into the jar of water, then gave the jar to the woman and told her to drink everything in it.

The Law of Moses said if she was guilty, "her people will reject her. But if the woman has not sinned, she is pure....she will be able to have babies" (Numbers 5:27-28 NCV).

Some scholars speculate that this law was more about protecting the woman from a violently jealous husband than proving guilt. If drinking a jar of dirty water would placate him, the argument goes, that was better than a beating.

WHAT HAPPENED TO UNWANTED CHILDREN
IN NEW TESTAMENT TIMES?

Unwanted children, whether Roman or Jewish, had a slim chance of finding a happy ending and growing up as an adopted child of someone who loved them.

Sadly, it was more likely, especially among Romans, that their story ended one of these ways:

- Death at birth by strangulation, drowning, sacrifice to a god, or exposure from being abandoned.
- Found abandoned at birth and raised as a family slave, a money-making prostitute, or a human asset sold to the highest bidder. Some locations became known as drop sites for newborns. People who wanted a child kept an eye on these places.
- Adopted and raised as an apprentice to help with a family's business.
- Public assistance. Emperor Trajan (reigned AD 98–117) supported around 145 boys and 34 girls. Scholars suggest there were fewer girls because the others were killed at birth.

Most Jewish writers in New Testament times condemned abortion and infanticide. "Raise your own child and don't kill it," said first-century Jewish historian Josephus. "The Immortal is angry at anyone who commits these sins."

Jews often raised abandoned children they found. So rabbis developed rules to guide the adoptive parents. If the newborn child was a circumcised boy, properly massaged in olive oil and powdered, one rabbi suggested treating him as Jewish and not as a "foundling."

If the child was a girl, there was no way of knowing if she was Jewish. So she wasn't allowed to marry a true-born Jew. But she could marry someone who converted to the Jewish faith.

Scholars estimate that only about half the newborn children of the Roman Empire lived to age five. With such high mortality rates, scholars say many parents resisted going all in on a child; the mom and dad withheld their emotional attachment until well into their offspring's childhood.

Imported, perfumed oil of pure nard (also called spikenard, an essential oil derived from a relative of the valerian family, grown in the Himalayas), beautifully packaged in an alabaster stone jar holding around 12 ounces or half a liter), costing one year's salary. That describes the oil an unidentified woman brought to Jesus when He came to Bethany a few days before His crucifixion. "She opened the jar and poured the perfume on Jesus' head" (Mark 14:3 NCV).

Scholars speculate that one reason the perfume was so expensive is that perfumers made it from nard roots harvested and imported from Kashmir and Nepal, in the Himalayas. From those mountain valleys to Bethany, it's about 3,000 miles (4,800 kilometers) along dangerous caravan routes through what are now Iran, Iraq, and Syria.

Perfumers who created that kind of merchandise, highly sought and risky to transport, often lived the high life of the wealthy. These perfumers, who were sometimes members of a local guild, also created less expensive but wonderfully aromatic perfumes from local resources such as lavender leaves, rose petals, cinnamon bark, anise seeds, and resin from trees—for the woodsy smell of both frankincense and myrrh.

In the time of Jesus's ministry, archaeological evidence suggests people kept their perfumed oil and dry spices in ivory containers, alabaster jars, baked clay jars, and wooden perfume boxes.

Recipes remained secret. The unique blend of scents made many perfumes hard to counterfeit. In a time before deodorant, and in a generally hot and dry land like the Middle East, perfume and spices helped mask body odor.

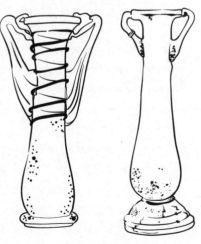

ANCIENT PERFUME CONTAINERS

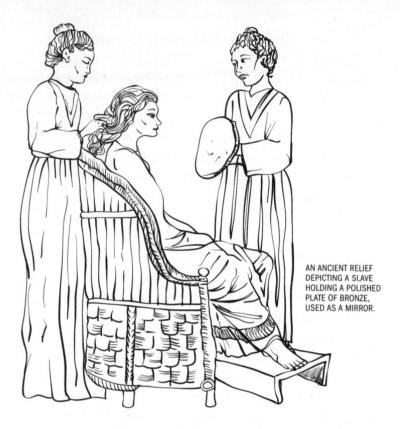

AN ANCIENT RELIEF
DEPICTING A SLAVE
HOLDING A POLISHED
PLATE OF BRONZE,
USED AS A MIRROR.

MAKEUP IN BIBLE TIMES

It seems even easier to understand the attraction to perfume after reading something written by the poet Horace (65 BC–8 BC). He reported that some women wore mud packs of crocodile dung to soften their skin and lighten their dark complexion. Who wouldn't want to come out of that smelling like roses?

Roman women in the first century used animal fat to lay a base for their makeup. Bear grease was a favorite. Women lightened their skin with powders ground from white minerals of lead, chalk, or a sedimentary rock called marl, also used as fertilizer. They added red to their cheeks with red ochre clay and red dye made from plants such as poppy petals. They colored their lips with lees, the leftover deposits of red wine.

Jewish women wore makeup too. Most evidence of this comes from containers found in graves and in ruins of destroyed villages. That includes Masada, a butte-topped fortress where a community of Jewish men, women, and children committed suicide rather than surrender to the Romans in AD 74.

Archaeologists found cosmetic palettes of limestone, along with cosmetic sticks for applying eye shadow and eyebrow liner. Those were made from soot mixed with animal fat and sometimes scented with saffron or another fragrance that didn't smell like a campfire.

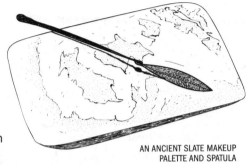

AN ANCIENT SLATE MAKEUP PALETTE AND SPATULA

Long eyelashes were in fashion. Wrinkles were not. Romans bought swan fat to grease away the wrinkles. Some rich Romans loved the silky feel of a bath in donkey milk.

Nearly all Jews and everyone else in the region moistened their dry skin with some kind of oil, often made from olives, and scented to hide the aroma of a human working under the Middle Eastern sun.

AN ANCIENT ROMAN WOMAN APPLYING COLOR TO HER LIPS.

Fiction Author
CAROLE TOWRISS

An unapologetic Californian, Carole Towriss now lives just north of Washington, DC. She loves her husband, her four children, the beach, and tacos, though not always in that order. This is her eighth biblical fiction novel. In addition to writing, she binge-watches British crime dramas and does the dishes four times in one day. You can find her at caroletowriss.com.

Nonfiction Author
STEPHEN M. MILLER

Stephen M. Miller is an award-winning, bestselling Christian author of easy-reading books about the Bible and Christianity. His books have sold over 1.9 million copies and include *The Complete Guide to the Bible, Who's Who and Where's Where in the Bible,* and *How to Get Into the Bible.*

Miller lives in the suburbs of Kansas City with his wife, Linda, a registered nurse. They have two married children who live nearby.

Read on for a sneak peek of another exciting story
in the Ordinary Women of the Bible series!

HER SOURCE OF STRENGTH
RAYA'S STORY

by Jill Eileen Smith

Raya tucked her long dark hair into her scarf as she walked, her heart beating fast. She'd hurried from the house too quickly, she realized with sudden annoyance, and left the water jar outside the door. This would never do. But the thought of returning to listen to Karmela one more time made her pause mid-step. *Adonai, why is she such a frustration?*

"How long am I going to have to wait for the water?" Karmela's sarcasm had stung.

"I'm going now," Raya had said, turning to do just that, but she could not escape Karmela's final words.

"You know, if you got up before sunrise, we could feed our men properly so they wouldn't have to eat dried bread and cheese before they left to care for the sheep. Really, Raya, it's not like you have to do all of the preparation…"

Raya had reached her rooms and shut the door, cutting off Karmela's rant. Let her talk to herself, or perhaps Manoah's mother, Adah, would hear and stop her...

The memory still irritated her as she finished securing her unruly hair and glanced at the heavens. The urge to complain, to utter words she would never say, which she knew offended Adonai, rose within her. But she squelched the temptation to speak them. Her sister-in-law cared nothing for Adonai, yet her children grew up like olive plants around her father-in-law's table and were simply too perfect. Karmela did not flaunt them in front of her, for which Raya thanked Adonai. But her overall undesirable attitude and that subtle lift of her chin caused Raya's frustration to rise like a pot bubbling over.

Berating herself for her lapse, she turned to head back to the house for the water jar. She could not shirk her duty to gather the morning's water, lest Talia be forced to do the job both day and night. Since Karmela did most of the grinding and cooking—her choice as the oldest, though not the first, daughter-in-law of the household—it fell to Raya and Talia to draw the water and clean up after meals. That Ariel had married her before his older brothers had wed seemed to have made Karmela proud of her status. She needn't have been, for despite the order of marriage, nothing changed the rights of Manoah as Baruch's firstborn.

If Karmela could simply curb her tongue as she worked, stop judging Raya for her barrenness or making comments to Talia about the quality of her weaving, the household would know some measure of peace.

Why does she think herself better than us, Adonai? She does, doesn't she? Or am I simply jealous because she has sons who follow Your law and though I am the first daughter-in-law to marry into this family and the oldest among the women, I have not one child to carry on my husband's name?

She slowed her pace as she neared the house, intending to go unnoticed as she grabbed the jar and hurried toward the well. She would not risk another encounter with Karmela when dawn had barely risen. But even as she bore the thought, guilt assailed her. She should be kinder, less easily frustrated with the woman. She was family, after all.

Raya approached the rooms she shared with Manoah, grateful for this door that led outside, separate from the main rooms of the house of her in-laws. As it was, too many people and too many rooms filled the land they owned in their town of Zorah. But she wouldn't mind one more. Surely a small babe wouldn't take much space. They could fit his bed near their own at first, and Manoah could build another room for him as he grew. Just one child. She wouldn't ask for more. Just one to take away her shame…and to stop Karmela's haughty looks.

Oh Adonai, what I wouldn't give for a child! The prayer came often as she walked alone to the well. *I wish I understood why You give sons to a woman who does not trust in You, yet I am denied.*

She sighed. There she was complaining again. She hurried to grab the jar and stalked off, angry with herself. Could she not control her own feelings for even a single morning? What was wrong with her that she was so emotional of late and easily troubled?

"Raya, wait!" She heard Talia's call and almost ignored it. But the sound of the one sister-in-law she adored made her stop. She could not be unkind, despite her inner turmoil.

Talia caught up with her and drew a steadying breath, a water jar also held atop her head. "I thought we could walk together."

"But you gather this evening. You didn't need to come twice."

"Karmela asked for more, and Adah suggested I go with you. They are expecting guests tonight—at least that is what Elead told me before he left with Manoah to tend the flocks." Talia settled into step with Raya, who looked at her, assessing her. Talia was easy to talk to and her favorite of the women in Baruch's household. Frustrated or not, she suddenly welcomed the company.

"Visitors will make more work, but it will be nice to hear whatever news they bring."

"I think they are relatives from up in the hills, but Elead was not certain, and I didn't ask Adah. Of course, Karmela is running around barking orders and I didn't want to get in her way." She laughed, and Raya joined her.

"We really shouldn't tease about her," Raya said after a moment and another wave of guilt. "She does her best, and at least she enjoys doing most of the cooking."

Talia kept her eyes on the path, but she gave a slight nod. "I suppose, but you have to admit, it is good to laugh."

Raya held her tongue a moment before responding. "I know. You are right. I just would not want to be the person people laughed about. I already feel the watchful eye of Adah and I see her shake her head in disappointment that I have not borne Manoah a son. I will admit, today is not a good day for me." She swallowed, unable to say more.

Talia stopped and turned to face Raya. She placed one hand on her shoulder, the other still holding the jar atop her head. "You have done nothing wrong, Raya. You are too hard on yourself and I doubt very much that Adonai is upset with you for how you feel. If He would open your womb, He knows your feelings would change, so how can He blame you for feeling sad or frustrated with those who add to your shame?"

Raya tilted her head, scrunching her brows together. "Then you are saying I should blame Adonai for my barrenness?" She couldn't do that no matter what people said. The fault was hers. Either she had sinned or God had other reasons, but she would not blame Him. Could not fault Him. He gave life and breath and she would trust Him whether He gave her a child or not. Yet the yearning in her soul for a son did not abate, even with her determined conviction to be content with her life.

"No, I didn't mean it that way," Talia said, backtracking her words. "I would not fault God, but it does seem odd that He has not blessed you. So many women of old who were barren, the patriarchs' wives for example, all bore children who grew up to become great people. Perhaps God is going to do the same for you." She patted Raya's shoulder and then moved on toward the well.

Raya walked beside her, though her feet wanted to drag behind. Talia was wrong. Sarah, Rebekah, and Rachel were chosen…special to God. They were barren for a time but only because God had great reason and their offspring did great things. She was Raya, wife of Manoah from a tribe that wasn't even born of one of Jacob's wives, just a maidservant concubine. Dan—a tribe of such little significance, despite its connection to Rachel's maidservant.

God did not do miracles for barren women in obscure tribes like hers. And even if He did, for what purpose? What reason would He have for giving her a son now? What good could a son of hers do? She glanced heavenward, but the clouds scudding across the blue sky held no answers.

Face it, Raya. You may long for Adonai, but He does not notice you. You are nobody special and your child could do nothing for Israel. The Philistines control us. What can one child do? Even one with the greatest gifts and most strength cannot free us from a grasp of evil pagan worshippers who do all they can to oppress us.

Israel was getting what it deserved from the Philistine oppression, for everyone knew—those who still cared about God's laws—that most of Israel had done evil in His sight. They never learned, though oppressors always came when they fell away from God's ways.

She kicked a stone in the path. Forty years of this oppression seemed like forever, and people were weary of it all—*she* was weary of it all. But she couldn't do anything to stop their enemies any more than she could turn light to darkness. And any child she might bear certainly could do nothing. Israel needed a great leader and a large army, but the nation was too disjointed, like Raya's own thoughts and emotions.

They reached the well, and she shoved her longing thoughts aside. "I'm glad you came," she said, glancing at Talia. "Perhaps when we return, we can help Karmela for a change. If she will let us."

"She will let us this time, I think. At least until she has everything under control." Talia lowered her jar and pulled it up dripping and sweating along the sides. Raya did the same and the two began the trek homeward.

"I will do whatever she needs," Raya said, denying the kick of jealousy and guilty hope that Karmela would refuse her help and let her weave with Talia in peace. But as they approached the house and heard the commotion of children and Karmela shouting and Adah's voice adding to the clamor, Raya wished she could retract her promise to help and run to the fields to pray.

Sometimes a day did not go the way it should.

Raya slipped away from the house midafternoon to finally fulfill her longed-for time alone. The breeze whipped against the headscarf and she fought its force toward a copse of trees not far from home, yet far enough to drown out the noise of the household and allow her to think. At her approach, the branches swayed as if in greeting. She stepped into a clearing and the wind quieted but for the swish of the leaves. A turn toward the fields gave her a better view, but a moment later, a blinding light blocked her vision. She looked heavenward. Had the sun suddenly broken through her sanctuary and sent a shaft of its light to warm her?

The light moved, and a few moments later, she saw the outline of a man. The urge to scream rose in her throat but as the man grew visible, she knew this was no ordinary person. The glow encasing him was like that of an angel. His bearing and size, larger and taller than two men, sent her to her knees. Raya planted her face to the earth, and an uncontrollable shaking moved through her from head to toe. *Who are you?* Surely he was not of this world. Was she imagining him? If she opened her tightly shut eyes, would he disappear?

Raya. Had he called her name? She lifted her head, cautious, trembling. And then she was suddenly kneeling her gaze lifted upward, as if he had tipped her chin without her realizing it.

"Even though you have been unable to have children," the man said, his voice deep yet nearly a whisper in her ear, "you will soon become pregnant and give birth to a son. So be careful; you must not drink wine or any other alcoholic drink nor eat any forbidden food. You will become pregnant and give birth to a son, and his hair must never be cut. For he will be dedicated to God as a Nazirite from birth. He will begin to rescue Israel from the Philistines."

I'm going to have a son? She wanted to ask him aloud, but in a moment he disappeared, the light no longer blinding her. What had she witnessed? She glanced at the sky peeking through the trees. *Adonai?*

Surely the visit was from an angel of the Lord. Who but God could tell the future? Who but God would choose her son to be a Nazirite from birth? No other culture understood the call of a Nazirite. Had she dreamed him? But no. She had just entered the trees when he appeared.

You're going to have a child. A child. The thought overwhelmed her, and the sudden fear and joy of it rushed through her bringing the melody of song to her lips. *Praise You, Adonai! Praise be to Your Name!*

A tune accompanied her words as she moved from thinking to singing them aloud. She rose slowly and raised her hands to the sky. "How good You are, Adonai!"

She turned then toward the fields where Manoah kept the sheep, lifted her robe above her ankles, and ran toward him with all of her strength. If she were not thinking clearly, Manoah would set her straight and tell her she was tired, overwrought. But if she truly had seen the angel of the Lord, he would believe her words. Her praise would not be without merit.

She ran faster, her breath heaving. She was not sure she wanted to know what he would say, but she knew she would not rest until she told him all that had happened.

A NOTE FROM THE EDITORS

We hope you enjoy the Ordinary Women of the Bible series, created by the Books and Inspirational Media Division of Guideposts, a nonprofit organization that touches millions of lives every day through products and services that inspire, encourage, help you grow in your faith, and celebrate God's love in every aspect of your daily life.

Thank you for making a difference with your purchase of this book, which helps fund our many outreach programs to military personnel, prisons, hospitals, nursing homes, and educational institutions. To learn more, visit Guideposts Foundation.org.

We also maintain many useful and uplifting online resources. Visit Guideposts.org to read true stories of hope and inspiration, access OurPrayer network, sign up for free newsletters, download free e-books, join our Facebook community, and follow our stimulating blogs.

To learn about other Guideposts publications, including the bestselling devotional *Daily Guideposts*, go to ShopGuideposts.org, call (800) 932-2145, or write to Guideposts, PO Box 5815, Harlan, Iowa 51593.

Sign up for the Guideposts Fiction Newsletter

and stay up to date on the books you love!

You'll get sneak peeks of new releases, recommendations from other Guideposts readers, and special offers just for you . . . *and it's FREE!*

Just go to Guideposts.org/Newsletters today to sign up.

Guideposts®

Visit Guideposts.org/Shop or call (800) 932-2145

Find more inspiring stories in these best-loved Guideposts fiction series!

Mysteries of Lancaster County

Follow the Classen sisters as they unravel clues and uncover hidden secrets in Mysteries of Lancaster County. As you get to know these women and their friends, you'll see how God brings each of them together for a fresh start in life.

Secrets of Wayfarers Inn

Retired schoolteachers find themselves owners of an old warehouse-turned-inn that is filled with hidden passages, buried secrets, and stunning surprises that will set them on a course to puzzling mysteries from the Underground Railroad.

Tearoom Mysteries Series

Mix one stately Victorian home, a charming lakeside town in Maine, and two adventurous cousins with a passion for tea and hospitality. Add a large scoop of intriguing mystery, and sprinkle generously with faith, family, and friends, and you have the recipe for *Tearoom Mysteries*.

Mysteries of Martha's Vineyard

Come to the shores of this quaint and historic island and dig in to a cozy mystery. When a recent widow inherits a lighthouse just off the coast of Massachusetts, she finds exciting adventures, new friends, and renewed hope.

To learn more about these books, visit Guideposts.org/Shop